This book is a work of fiction. Any references to historical events, real people, or real places are used fictitiously.

RhomeStead Books

1st Edition

Text copyright 2024 Riley G. Powers
All rights reserved, including the right to reproduction in whole or in part in any form.

Edited by: Rose W. Fredette
Cover Design by: Tiffany June

ISBN: 979-8-218-43618-6

Get in touch with the author by emailing them at:
Powersgriley@gmail.com

For mature audiences only. Not suitable for children.
19+

Acknowledgments

I would first like to thank my friends and family who supported me through the entire writing process. To my partner for listening to me ramble and babble on and on through endless nights about the story. To my brother, for helping me realize that this was a tale worth telling. To Monkey–watching you write gave me the push I needed to finish a story that started as a joke. To our amazing editor who helped the story and text blossom to its true potential. To our artist who made the story come to life. And finally, to Lola Faust who gave me the courage to do something unexpected and erotic.

Summer with Sasquatch

Chapter 1

Summer woke to the prickly, rough nuzzling that was Harry's face stubble. A feature she found charming when it wasn't scratching her. Harry seemed to grow hair only on his face; the rest was a pale, milky-white palate that toned shapely in the right light.

"I got a big day today, babe." Hot breath bathed the back of her neck with a thickness only breaking a morning silence in bed can bring.

Summer of course knew what this meant and obliged as if conditioned. With sleepy eyes still closed, she pushed her ass back against the hardness that was Harry. Immediately, Summer felt Harry push back. Soft, but hard flesh found its way between Summer's round, plump backside that received her many compliments—a gesture by men she found they thought to be the new norm of chivalry.

"There's a good girl," Harry's raspy morning voice was followed by a swift swat to Summer's ass before he began groping where he had stuck her; kneading her soft round behind, peeling a cheek back momentarily before letting go to jiggle itself back into place. Harry's cock quickly found its way between these bubbly cheeks, snaking itself under her flossy black G-string. Summer hated wearing underwear that stayed up her butt all night, but Harry insisted on it. And what Harry wanted, Harry got. For now, at least.

"Let's make sure daddy has a good day, okay babe?" Harry kissed the back of Summer's neck. Their rhythmic grinding had pushed aside Summer's sanctioned G-string and allowed Harry's stiffness to find her soft, wet folds. Summer rarely had issues with arousal—either within herself or others--and found herself, more often than not, ready to indulge in whatever sexual act came next since she had left the small modest coastal town she called home and moved to the city. Here with the lights and the constant flow of people, Summer found a liberation she had never experienced. The dense forest that surrounded her small logging town had always offered her a sense of wildness, but the city's electricity had amplified her core.

A soft whimper escaped Summer's lips as she felt herself open to Harry when he pushed himself inside. Sliding out to the very tip of his cock head, then reentering her again, this time with a little more ease as his cock was coated in her wetness. In moments, Harry's erection was rhythmically flexing itself, the speed quickening as he thrust himself inside Summer, their bodies colliding aggressively. She could feel his dick rubbing against her g-spot with each violent thrust.

"Messy girl," he smugly whispered. Summer could feel the devilish grin on Harry's face as the wet, gushy sound from her creaming pussy and his unrelenting member filled the quiet room. She didn't have to look down to know that she was thoroughly soaked and no doubt, Harry's sex would be covered by her fluids, running down both their bodies to form a puddle under them.

Summer's creased eyebrows joined in the middle of her forehead, as she pushed back on Harry's stiff rod with her lower body, allowing the arch of him to fill her completely. She felt herself let go simultaneously as her body tightened, the aftershock coursing through her. Harry had no problem making Summer cum, and he knew it. She found herself becoming increasingly irritated by his use of such a skill, as he used it, she felt, to his advantage and not hers. It was if it were a game—a rigged hand that he always won that stroked his already inflated ego. She gripped the bedsheets, eyes shut hard as her juices continued to surge on Harry's erection as it bucked in and out of her.

"Did my girl just cream on this cock?" Harry asked with a hint of mockery behind his voice. Without warning he reached over her and grasped her nipple between his fingers and pinched them. Softly at first. Then harder, seeing the effect it was having on her as she gasped out her answer.

"Such a good girl," Harry smirked through his words. "Now clean up the mess you made and milk this dick." A quick slap on Summer's ass and Harry rolled over onto his back, his glistening phallic departing her still quivering pussy as it towered, a false idol in the sunshine that crept through the window, glistening in the light. Panting slightly, Summer gathered herself together and obeyed.

"Just look at that mess," Harry smirked again as he watched Summer get up and crawl between his legs towards his cream-coated cock.

"Now, you give that dick a nice fat kiss and tell him thank you," Harry sneered, enjoying handing out directions to Summer. Summer puckered her lips and kissed the mocking head. A small rope of her juices dangled from the head to her lips as she looked up at Harry.

"Thank you," she purred with a voice she knew he loved, before kissing it again, and again until she was making out with it. Tongue lolling over the sticky prickhead while her left hand milked him at the base.

"Yes, that's a good girl," Harry sighed watching her. "Make daddy cum baby," he encouraged her by reaching down and pushing the back of her head, forcing his thick base into her mouth and down her throat.

A muffled cry of surprise followed from Summer's filled mouth as she instinctively began bobbing her head up and down his prick, dragging her tongue and lips along the shaft. Spit and pre cum began leaking from her lips as she continued to milk him.

"Come on babe, you can do better than that," Harry growled, pushing her head down hard, forcing inch after inch down her throat while maintaining her bouncing head. Her eyes watered as she looked up at his sly, smug face.

"There it is," he sighed. She could feel his rod flexing, growing, straining to release itself inside her. Harry let out a long groan and Summer felt the warm and salty liquid fill the back of her throat, then her mouth before she quickly swallowed what she could. Sitting up, dribbles of cum leaked from her lips as she gulped the rest before looking at Harry for praise.

Harry was quick to rise out of bed and stretch his arms up over his head giving a big fake lion's roar that was ill-suited for his human body.

"Dam, babe. I really needed that." And with a quick and unapologetic wink, his pale buttocks left the room to get ready for his big day, leaving Summer in the tussled sheets.

Hot water streamed down onto Summer's face as she showered alone with her thoughts. She was happy with Harry, she told herself—he was the distraction she'd been looking for. He could be demanding and chauvinist at times, and, well, kind of a douche. But he had his redeeming qualities as well. For one, he could always make her orgasm. And after the last few underwhelming performances from boyfriends Summer had been with, that in itself was a huge accomplishment. But, there was always something. Even after having amazing sex, Summer was left with something that wasn't being filled. Arguably, it was hard to fit anything else into their relationship with the size of Harry's ego. Summer smiled smugly at her snide thought and closed her eyes under the heat and steam that enwrapped her body and held her close. Small bubbles of suds danced across the curve of her breast as she washed the morning sex off her. The white, playful foam found its way cascading down her shape. Summer ran her hands along her skin using the hot water to rinse away the soap, leaving behind a silky smooth texture she couldn't resist.

Her breast, slippery from the suds, perked up as her fingertips drew small circles across her nipples. She had always thought her nipples were cute: small, and pink, they almost always gave her feelings away. Her fingers continued to trace down, enjoying the velvety sensation on the underside of her breast as she cupped and cradled herself in the moment. Summer gently and quickly flitted down her stomach with her fingers before they found themselves skating over her bare wet mound. Hot-pink from the heat, Summer's opening warmly welcomed the length of her middle finger, as she began to caress herself. She ran her finger up, down and in between her lips, pushing deeper in each time, feeling her wetness begin to mix with the shower's own ejaculate. Her glistening finger rolled up once more before finding her clit. A smile spread across Summer's face as she applied pressure under her hood, her other hand reaching out to steady herself against the shower wall. Eyes pinched tight, Summer's finger began to flex in small, slow circles, edging around her hood.

"Fuck," Summer sighed enjoying herself, alone in this small space with just her body and the hot water endlessly streaming over her. Her finger quickened and tightened its small rings around her most sensitive spot before she added her pointer finger to the mix. Summer's body arched and strained from the feeling, her face looking up straight into the pouring hot water. Faster and faster. Her two fingers began to play her soft flesh like a mad musician, never stopping or slowing, as a warm sensation, deep inside her, growing and growing, growling to be let out, to be freed. Summer's mouth gaped open, hot water crashing against her tongue, emitting no noise in fear that Harry would hear and know what she was doing.

With a slight arch to her fingers and just a push of more pressure, Summer's knees bent slightly from the overwhelming sensation that had grabbed her from the inside and spun her around and around.

Summer breathed out quickly, nearly gasping for the next breath she'd been holding as her glory orgasmed and gushed quietly with the downpour of the shower. Her fingers clawed at the tile of the wall as her knees buckled again briefly before she was able to regain herself. Straightening up and giggling with a small grin, she allowed her fingers to trace back up her stomach and her chest one more time. She captured this small moment in her mind. *A moment for me*, she thought to herself. *No one knows me better than I do, not even Harry.*

Summer shut the water off and stood for a moment, allowing the water to slowly bead off her body. The final wisp of steam left her soft skin the moment the last of her dreamy sensation ceased. The warmth between her legs turned cold when the shower curtain opened, and forced her back into reality.

"Dude, get the fuck outta here!" Harry's excitement met Summer as she came wrapped in her towel back to the bedroom. She sat on the sex-messed bed looking quizzically up at Harry who was pacing the room with a bounce in his step, phone pushed hard against his ear.

"Dude, I am *there*! I would not miss this!"

Harry was well-liked, both at work and social networks. It wasn't uncommon for their plans to be interrupted by a friend of Harry's who'd spotted them. Sometimes evenings out would turn into a carousel of detours when his buddies would tell him where they were drinking that evening or where they should venture to next. Summer didn't mind, for the most part. It was not a lifestyle she was used to but figured this is just what city-couples did.

It was incredible, at first, the amount of people who knew Harry; they'd even run into his acquaintances at the grocery store. So much for getting swept up in the huge sea of a city. One of the reasons Summer had left her small, never-changing town was exactly for that reason: she wanted to be lost in the crowd, anonymous--somewhere where no one knew her name, or face. Somewhere that no one could stop her to lament once more on the tragedy that had taken her father not too long ago. Selfishly, she wanted to put as much distance away as she could from her old life. Summer had found that distractions were a sedative to her mourning and grief.

The day she had received the news of her father's passing, Summer had turned into the town's self-proclaimed caretaker. She would wake in the morning with a list of errands she needed to run for her elderly neighbor, volunteer for a highway clean-up crew, or babysit for the new family in town. She preferred doing anything, it seemed, except stopping to accept the truth. Whenever she would stop to reflect, all she could see was her father: A forest ranger, in his dulled green uniform, lying where they found him in the quiet woods with a felled tree near him. The incident was deemed an accident, the cause of death was severe blunt force trauma to his head.

Her boyfriend, at the time of her father's death, had tried to be helpful, but had the maturity level of a pygmy goat and failed miserably in any of his attempts to be supportive.

"You gotta slow down Summer. Like, your dad just died, and you haven't even cried yet," he had voiced to her in a fashion that left his face scrunched and folded.

"I'm fine," she remembered saying with a fake grin. "They need me right now, I can't just stop because something shitty happened. Then what would happen to them? He was always taking care of this town. Now it's my turn." Looking back, Summer realized that was the first lie she told herself, with many more to come.

Her boyfriend had let out a sad sigh, then moved to kiss her, his mouth quickly going for her tongue. *Wow really, that quick huh?* She had gone along with it because she was too nice to stop him. When his long, skinny fingers crept up her shirt and under her bra she pulled back and shoved him.

"What the fuck Mark! You honestly think *this* is the best time to be feeling up my tits?" She got up from the porch bench and made to go inside when Mark grabbed her by the wrist.

"Come on Summer... We haven't fooled around in like, a few days. Besides, you really could use the distraction." He began pulling her back towards him when a low, guttural growl came from the steps leading to the porch.

"What's going on here?" Both Summer and Mark's heads snapped to the voice. A giant of a man stood there, barrel-chested, and bearded with a frame much sturdier than the feeble hands that were slowly relinquishing their grip on Summer.

"We...we were just messin' around," Mark stammered, as his eyes looked down. "I think I'm gonna go. I'll hit you up later Summer." Mark left quickly, not brave enough to shoot a second glance at Summer or the burly stranger as he scurried down the steps.

The man chuckled. "Boys, think they're God's gift to women." He walked up the stairs mechanically, big worn steel-toed boots clapping down on each step. He settled himself on the porch bench and looked up at Summer.

"How you doin' kiddo?" His eyes, so soft and gentle compared to his brutish body wavered and flickered up to her.

Summer closed her eyes tightly and shook her head, fighting desperately to keep the tears from escaping. She felt a hand on her wrist. This time, however, even though it was big and calloused, its touch was tender against her skin. He did not pull her. He simply helped her gently, and she could feel a wave of warmth pass from him to her.

Ben had been her father's best friend and partner in the forest service. Growing up, Summer only had her father. Her mother had left shortly after Summer's birth and besides her, there was no other real family to speak of. Ben, in many ways, had been like a secondary father to her. He sat next to her, resembling a lumberjack with this flannel shirt and Carhartt beanie. Summer glanced up and caught herself looking at the thick black chest hair that peeked from his open collar. This feature of Ben had always left her feeling intrigued—although it was never a sexual curiosity. She merely found it beautiful in a way that always left her wondering why.

"I just picked this up from the funeral home." Ben presented a small metal flask into Summer's palm. It was her father's flask—a familiar object where he had always kept his favorite whisky that kept him warm during the wintry seasons in the woods. The only thing that filled it now was ashes of his remains. Summer swelled as she took it with trembling hands.

"You know kiddo, it wouldn't hurt to get away for a while. Start a new chapter. This place ain't the same without your dad, we both know that." She nodded as she rocked, holding the flask close to her.

"Filling his shoes around here won't fill that empty spot you got for him. Take a break. Explore the world a bit, the way he explored the forest. And for God's sake, find a new boyfriend." He chuckled as Summer found herself laughing, despite the hot tears that she so desperately wanted to force out.

"You're right," she agreed, examining the flask for any remaining fingerprints that might have belonged to her father.

She kissed the cool metal to her lips. "But it doesn't mean I have to do it alone."

Chapter 2

"You will not fucking believe this!" Harry exclaimed wildly as he began tapping on his phone like a madman. "Byron got tickets to tomorrow night's game!" His smile stretched up to meet his ears as he glanced at Summer quickly before returning his attention to the screen. Summer's face immediately puckered with irritability.

"Uh, as in, tomorrow, tomorrow? You realize we have a trip planned right?" The loaded backpacks in the corner mocked her with their wide zippered smiles.

Harry froze for a moment, then, without missing a beat, blurted out, "Babe, we can go backpacking any weekend we want. This game won't happen again!" His body was turned toward her, eyes wide and pleading like a guilty child trying to avoid punishment. Summer crossed her arms and shook her head in disbelief.

"Hey." His fingers roped through hers as he knelt down to eye level with her, his charm-adorned-clogs cranking away, while his eyes flashed her his best puppy-dog look. "This is a once in a lifetime experience babe. An experience we get to share, together!"

It was amazing to Summer how quickly Harry would become the quintessential Dennis Quaid rom-com sweetheart the instant his options included other dudes, sports, and booze. A smirk bounced off Summer's lips as she stood, moving to their closet to find herself an outfit.

"Have fun." Her towel dropped, revealing her beautifully sculpted legs and rounded backside.

"What? You're not coming?" Harry's expression was the one that reared its head when being told, "no".

"We had plans, Harry. And not just date night plans, but plans that mean something to me." She glanced at the metal flask standing on the dresser. "You know how important this trip is to me. This is where I want to scatter my dad's ashes. Don't you understand what this means to me?" Coat hangers clinked along the metal line as she roused through them, looking for the long sleeve she planned on wearing.

"Babe, come on!" Almost begging now, Harry scooted over to her, still on his knees while gripping her with both hands on her still-warm bottom. "I promise, pinky promise, that we'll go next weekend. Just you and me…please!" He began kissing her round cheeks. Summer sighed. While she slightly enjoyed his pleading, she was also turned off by his groveling. But, she figured she could use his clear desperation to her advantage.

"I'm going on this trip, with or without you. I really don't give a fuck what you do Harry, but I need this and I'm going." She abruptly turned around, interrupting his kiss-ass smooching. Her hour-shaped body stood before him, one of her meticulously groomed eyebrows arched, and a look of pure disappointment in her eyes.

"Are you gonna be mad if I stay and go to the game? I promise we'll go on a hike, or something next weekend. I promise babe." His hands had found their way around her butt once again and he pulled her hips toward his face. "Please, babe, don't be mad. Maybe it'll be good for you to do a 'you' thing this weekend. Ya know, just like all those backpacking trips you said you and your dad would go on when you were younger" His lips dragged up along her inner thigh. His nose nuzzled into her lower stomach. She could feel his hot breath rolling off her skin.

Summer's mind wandered back to all those trips with her father. The excitement of returning each year to their secret spot in the Cascades. Her father used to beam, telling others that he had backpacked in on this particular trail before Summer had hit her first year. "Thought she'd wake up in the middle of the night and wake up Bigfoot with her cries, but this lil' adventurer slept straight on through the night up there." She could picture his warm, genuine smile now. So proud of her and the bond and all the memories they had created together. Summer felt a sudden lurch of guilt, having abandoned the tradition when she became too "cool" to venture out with her dad. The regret of not going that one last trip before his untimely death gnawed at her, the same way a Spruce Beetle eats its way through a tree.

"Yeah, maybe you're right," Summer doled out, her fucks long given and gone. "Go with your friends. It's a 'once-in-a-lifetime thing'." She wondered if the mockery showed. but she was determined to use the situation to her advantage. "And maybe…" Her smirk returned as her hand pushed the back of Harry's head, forcing his face between her freshly washed legs, a dominant gesture she rarely flexed. "And maybe, you can show me how sorry you are for ditching me this weekend." A coy smile spread across her lips as she enjoyed the position of power she held over him for once.

His response was soundless, but clear as she felt his warm, wet tongue roll up and in between her shaven folds. The tip of his tongue missed her clit completely, a maneuver she was not unaccustomed to by now. His tongue swiveled and whiplashed frantically everywhere except where it needed to land; when it came to the appreciation of women's oral pleasure, he was but a baby, stumbling in the dark. Long exhales bellowed out of him like dragon's fire, overcompensating for his lack of expertise.

His tongue was merely a sopping wet sponge, dabbing and dousing her sex with a mild fervor. Back and forth, up and down, faster and faster. It reminded her of a wiggling fish on a hook—it had no idea of what was happening. Summer's eyes shut tightly as she reached and gripped the closet's door frame for support, feigning dramatics to urge him on. The hand that was on her ass slipped under her thigh, pushing her legs apart before gliding up to find her pussy drenched from all his slobber. It was easy for him to slide his middle finger inside her as he continued lapping her up. His finger arched as it slid in and out of her in a chaotic rhythm. *Finally*, she thought as she felt her body tighten and relax at the same time. An authentic gasp and whimper fled from Summer's mouth as she felt herself ready to let go on Harry's face.

"Yes. Oh my god yes Harry, right there." Her knees began to buckle expecting more to come when the sound of Harry's phone barged its way into space. Harry suddenly stopped and stood, wiping his wet face with the back of his hand and grinning like the devil.

"You'll get the rest of your apology when you get back," he winked and went back for his phone, leaving Summer standing stripped of her clothes and dignity, but not shocked. She shook her head in disbelief and knew then and there that her and Harry were done.

Chapter 3

Summer's beat-up Subaru rolled up and over the mountain pass with ease and Summer found herself on the eastern side of the state much more quickly than expected. She had fled the apartment before Harry left, leaving for her trip earlier than planned in frustration and passively avoiding the break-up conversation that was to come with her return. A small picture of her father, bearded and flannelled in a small frame, swung from her rearview mirror. Aside from her father smiling down on her, a spooky podcast accompanied her as she drove. Fueled by the memory of a soon to be idiot ex-boyfriend, time seemed to fly out the window and into the clear air as she drove through the mountain-scape.

The spooky podcast, however, may not have been the best idea. Monstrous creatures looming in the hills and abducting unknowing backpackers was not the way she wanted to start her solo journey. The idea of creatures lurking in the trees caused her to pull out her phone to send a text to her manager. Seeing as Harry was the only one who knew she was making this trip, and her only friends were friends of Harry, she decided to play it safe and let at least one person know where she was going. She shot off a quick text:

Hey Valerie. I'm taking a quick backpacking trip up past Hyas Lake for the weekend. Wanted to let someone know in case Bigfoot kidnaps me lol Hope you have a great weekend!

The indication of the sent bar paused midway, a result of the shoddy reception and technology the wilderness did not condone. Summer had landed her marketing job through, yet again, a connection of Harry's. She had surprised herself at how quickly she excelled in the advertising department. She seemed to have a quick knack for knowing what people wanted— a trait, she realized, that may have just been what trapped her with Harry.

She found her exit on the freeway, past the last lake reservoir that nestled under the slopes of the pass now behind her. There was still that creepy-ass gas station, jarring at the roundabout as she made her way into the old mining town of Roslyn.

Jeez, that thing is still there? Summer tensed as her eyes locked on the decrepit gas station. The telling signs of age and decay had been apparent, even while she was a child and her father had taken her this way for their first backpacking trip all those years ago.

"That place is so creepy!" She would whine behind her hands shielding her eyes as they drove past.

"You can't keep up on the trail, I'll have to bring you back here to stay the night," he joked with her, dark humorous eyes looking back at her startled face in the rearview mirror.

"You would not!" Her gasp rose with her body, daring to peak up to get a better look at the building, covered in peeling paint and weeds.

"It's scary! You couldn't pay me a million bucks to stay there!"

Her father chuckled. "You know, there's a good many things in this world that look scary, but I always found the more I know about something, the more I know the story behind it, the less fear I have. Why don't you give that scary station a story. See if you're still scared the next time we come up here."

Years would pass, yet each trip they made, the gas station was still there, greeting them like the old aunt you don't want to hug at your birthday party. Her big fake smile and flabby arms trying to trap you in with all the secrets she's kept. Summer would find herself making up stories about the place. She'd often invent a new story each time they made their way past it. Her favorite was the story of the lovers: a young newlywed couple from the city that had moved out here to slow down for a change; people who were tired of the noise and technology and wanted to build their future with their hands. The kind who thought keeping chickens was cute and fun and tried each year to cultivate produce but ended up misguided by planting broccoli in the summer heat and bok choy in full sun. A bit naïve, sure, but that's why Summer loved them—they were real and didn't mind making mistakes or failing. For them, it was enough that they had each other, and they were doing IT. Whatever 'it' was, Summer didn't know. She had invented their love, but she herself had not experienced such. Yet there they were in her mind, buying this gas station from an older couple who were ready to retire and take their new RV on the road and out of Roslyn.

There had been an accident. In her mind, Summer saw a terrible fire consuming them one night in their sleep due to a fault in the station's piping. She liked the idea of them going that way: together and doing what they wanted to do. Not afraid to fail. She admired them in their nonexistence; their love that inspired each other to live.

This did not make the station any less scary, however, and Summer drove by it, realizing that she did so for the first time alone.

Chapter 4

As the paved road wound its way lazily around lakes, and loud rivers, slowly creeping its way back up the forested slopes of the mountains, Summer reluctantly rolled up her windows as it turned to gravel and dry dust. Her car inclined forward as she made the slow ascent up the narrow road towards the trailhead. She never could get over how two miles of road could be stretched into over an hour of driving. She enjoyed the slow crawl however, slowing down to admire a cabin off the road, or a view over a sheer cliff. The forest, vast and mysterious, made her think of her father. Summer had not been on this small gravel road for years and she noticed how narrow it had become since her last visit, erosion eating at the edge. Her hands gripped the wheel of the car as she thought what would happen should another car come along the other way, but forced the negative thought away, focusing on not driving over any particularly large rocks protruding from the dusty earth.

Even with the dust stirring up around her car, the views were breathtaking. Summer couldn't help but look and breathe in the sight of the ancient forest out her driver-window and the raging river down below to her right.

The trailhead was easy to find, even if this was her first time driving to it without the guidance of her father, as it sat nestled in the trees where the dirt road ended. The now dust-covered Subaru pulled into the makeshift gravel and dirt parking lot up along the mountain meadowed hillside. Rotting stumps and large moss-covered rocks made for parking space markers, and she was surprised to see it so full. At least twenty cars, mostly Subarus, were occupying this quiet place where the last of civilization meets nature. Summer had always suspected this place was somewhat a secret when her father would take her. So often they would arrive to find this space empty, devoid of anyone except for themselves.

Summer nervously wondered if there would be any available spots along the lake to camp, let alone their secret spot they set up camp at.

"Well, we made it Dad," Summer brightly smiled at the small flask on the passenger seat.

Thick, hot air weighed down on Summer the moment she opened the car door and stepped onto the uneven ground. Summer looked around and her senses were instantly hit with an overwhelming surge of memories: hot pine needles, layering on top of one another, season after season; the constant hum and buzz of insects dancing with the mountain flowers; the sight of the dusky-green moss hanging from old growth branches, long and serpentine.

"Witch's hair," her dad had teased when she first laid eyes on these otherworldly sights. He had once collected enough of the moss and had bundled it atop his head, cackling like a witch as they laughed around an evening fire.

"Actually," her dad mused, pulling the lime-colored moss from his head, "this here is Sasquatch's favorite snack. *Nom nom nom.*" Summer giggled, watching her father pretend to eat the stringy green. "Other than children that is." He playfully reached for her with a dramatic growl.

"Dad! Stopppp!" She squealed, closing her blanket around her.

Her father's chuckles echoed between the trees.

"Don't you worry baby girl. If Mr. Bigfoot wanted to eat us he would've done it already. No, the big guy is a guardian of the forest. He would never harm you." Her father's stories of the mythical beast would grow more elaborate with each trip up the mountains, until the elusive being became a staple of fuel to their crackling campfires.

Summer's child imagination ran wild with the thought of such a mysterious creature who was capable of looking monstrous yet being a protector. Try as she might however, Sasquatch in her mind was just like the decrepit gas station—a story that brought both a smile and fear.

As Summer took a deep breath, absorbing everything in the stillness of the makeshift parking lot, she felt like she was home.

Her euphoric state was interrupted abruptly by the sound of bushes moving in front of her parked car. Summer had become accustomed to small critters rustling around the forest floor, but whatever was trailing its way toward her was no small critter. The sound of large, padded feet crescendoed to accompany the swaying of bushy leaves as they shuffled closer to her.

Summer felt frozen, unsure how to respond in the first minute of her grand adventure by herself. Before she even had time to chastise herself for being so unprepared and frightened, a large head, covered in black fur emerged from the brush and charged at her.

Summer nearly let out a squeak of simultaneous excitement and fear as the enormous Newfoundland dog trotted towards her. Curious and friendly, the shaggy dog sniffed at Summer's thigh before giving it a quick lick with its scratchy tongue.

"Atlas! Come here boy!" A woman's voice rang out through the parking lot. The giant dog bounded like a rabbit and sprinted off towards the voice.

Summer laughed at herself for a moment, her tense shoulders relaxing as she shook her head and moved around to the back of the Subaru to collect her overstuffed backpack. As Summer leaned into the trunk of the car, the same voice that had called for the dog sang behind her.

"Well, now I know why Atlas was so distracted." Summer could hear the smirk in her voice, but was undoubtedly happier that this sort of comment came from a woman instead of a man, which was usually so often the case.

Summer, grinning despite the direct comment, stood and turned to face a woman decked out in hiking gear. Despite the fact that her body was completely covered by activewear, Summer couldn't help but think how beautiful she was. She looked a bit older than Summer, slightly taller too, with short hair that slipped out under her Seattle Mariners cap. She stood with her hands on her hips, body cocked to one side in a stance of confidence that Summer found both intriguing and intimidating Her bright smile lit up with the mountain sun, and Summer couldn't help but mirror her warm gesture.

"Is he yours?" Summer asked, directing her eyes away from the woman's beautiful face to the large dog sitting by her side.

"This is Atlas," the woman said, reaching down to scratch the Newfoundland's oversized head. Atlas's tongue lolled out lazily as he looked up at her, a massive fluffy tail wagging behind him. "I hope he didn't scare you. He likes to wander off and find pretty things." Summer felt her face flush but decided to blame it on the sun's heat as it sizzled overhead.

"Sorry, I can be super forward. I'm Skyy. Two y's," she said, reaching out her hand. Summer took it, feeling how soft it was compared to Harry's.

"Summer," she said, shaking Skyy's hand. "Two m's," she said, giggling at her own stupid joke.

Atlas let out a low bark and nudged Skyy's free hand.

"Nice to meet you, Summer, with two m's." Skyy let go and went back to scratching Atlas's head. "He can be very needy at times, and a bit overprotective," Skyy said more to Atlas than to Summer, as she dropped her face to his slobbering snout. "Aren't you? Aren't you a needy boy?"

"Sounds like most men I know," Summer scoffed dryly.

"Truth girl. That's why I switched to the other team." Skyy looked up to gauge Summer's reaction, then quickly added a laugh. "Sorry, told you I was forward." Skyy eyed Summer's bulging backpack. "Speaking of being forward, are you about to hike in? Atlas and I are heading up to Trap Lake to meet up with my brother." Skyy surveyed the quiet parking area briefly. "There was a group of douchey looking frat guys who headed in right as I pulled up. Loud as fuck, and wearing those stupid ass visors. God I hate those things." Atlas responded with a low bark. "So does Atlas," Skyy laughed, rubbing the dog's head. "I'm all for woman empowerment and all that, but if you're comfortable with it, it'd make Atlas and me feel a bit better if we had another person with us on the trail."

Summer was caught off guard and began a mental debate with herself. Skky noted her reserve and hesitation.

"If not, totally okay. Not trying to be weird or stalkerish." Skky offered, withdrawing back a bit.

"Oh, no, I mean, yeah, let's do it," Summer was surprised at how quickly she obliged to the request and blamed Harry in the moment. "Now that you say that, I feel sorta dumb coming up here by myself. It's just, it's been something I've been meaning to do for a while now, and, I guess I didn't really think everything through." Summer glanced at her exposed legs that were to be subject to all of nature's many elements.

"Oh girl you're fine. I get it. Sometimes the best experiences are those that we don't plan for. I was so not ready to adopt this lug of fur when I got him, but look at us now. We're like an old married couple." Skyy's laughter brought Atlas to nudge her side before trotting off towards the trailhead. "Looks like that's our cue." Skyy cinched up her shoulder straps and turned to follow Atlas.

"Yeah, right behind you," Summer called as she gathered her things, closed the trunk, and returned to the passenger side door quickly to grab the small silver flask.

Chapter 5

Summer was astonished at how little the trail had changed over these many years. Each step was as if she was stepping into a calendar photo. She couldn't contain her grin at each familiar trickling creek, the makeshift wooden steps formed by back country trail builders, the smell of swamp mixed with hot pine. Their small group was quiet for the most part. Skyy trudged ahead at a faster pace than Summer was prepared for, and Summer was quickly sweating in the August heat that pierced through the trees. She regretted not wearing pants, as insects of all sorts found her bare legs the moment she stepped onto the worn trail path.

Skyy made small talk every so often, turning to show Summer an edible plant or remark on the wide dry riverbed they crossed. "This part always reminded me of the Elephants' graveyard from *The Lion King*." Skyy grinned as they clambered over the dry boulders. Summer had to agree that the pale dusty rocks that snaked their way down the mountainside and into their path did resemble massive bones.

It was clear that Skky was a seasoned hiker. Summer watched in amazement as Skyy would slip her hand slowly to brush against the foliage that spilled its way into the trails path, and like the quick peck of a bird, would pluck a small red Salmon berry hidden from Summer's view.

"Nature's candy," Skyy smiled, tossing the first treasure back to Summer.

Summer was surprised at how quickly she had reached her destination. She immediately recognized her dad's hidden spot when the large misshapen rock appeared next to the trail—she had always thought it looked like a laughing face when she was younger. Moss had claimed the rock, and the laughing face now resembled a chia pet, its facets covered in dark green fur.

"I think this is me," Summer panted, peering behind the rock to find a small overgrown path leading behind it towards the river.

"Already?" Skyy asked, looking slightly disappointed from her workout being cut short.

"Yeah…I was pretty young when my dad started to take me up here, so I wasn't able to go in that far. This just sorta became our place even once I got older to go further" Summer noticed the disappointment in Skyy's face. "Join me for lunch?" She beamed, leading the way past the rock without waiting for Skyy's response.

"Atlas! Come!" Skyy sounded out, following Summer with an eager smile.

The small path led them a short distance between ferns and fallen logs until they popped out from the brush onto a small sandy beach that hugged the river. The river was wide, nestled in between two slopes of mountain. Its slow flow and near transparency gave it the sense of a lake rather than a river. From the shore, large dark trees could be seen sleeping on their sides at the bottom of the water, looking like matches spilled from a long-forgotten box.

"Wow. I never knew this little beach was here," Skyy remarked, dropping her bag onto the beach looking around in wonder.

"This was my dad's secret spot. He used to tell me he was the only one who knew about it. '*Not even Bigfoot knows about this beach*,'" she laughed, mustering up the best impression she could of her best dad voice.

"Girl, Bigfoot def knows about this spot. If you see him, tell him to holler at me. I've been looking for him for years." Skyy dug her hand into her pocket and produced a small edible gummy, individually wrapped in plastic that showcased a marijuana leaf and Washington's "21+ years and older" indicator. "Do you indulge?" she asked, proffering the weed treat to Summer. "I usually smoke it, but, ya know, being high with a lit J in the woods might not the best idea." Skyy giggled, popping a gummy into her mouth.

Summer hesitated for a moment before shrugging her shoulders. "Sure, why not." Summer took the other gummy and savored the earthy-grape flavor. Summer wasn't unaccustomed to pot, but she only smoked on occasion due to how little it took her to get stuck-on-the-couch-high. *It's called Indica because you in-da-couch*, her dad used to laugh. A loud splash brought her attention back to the scenery. Skyy had quickly stripped down to her sports bra and briefs, racing and diving into the clear water. She dipped for a moment, then reappeared, catching her breath and turning towards Summer.

"Get your ass in here, it feels amazing!" she hollered, wading further in the water.

Summer couldn't help but grin and feel childish as she dropped her pack and looked around before lifting her shirt over her head.

"Ahhhoww!" Skyy called from the water, grinning.

"Oh my god, whatever," Summer laughed shimming out of her shoes and shorts before plunging into the cold water. The girls swam out towards a large tree trunk that was cresting the surface of the water at a delicate angle that was perfect for lounging on. Hoisting themselves onto the slick trunk, they sat in nature's silence. Gravity pulled the snow-melted water towards them and the trunk, breaking at the tip to roll along the tree's side and the girl's bare feet. Atlas watched them from the beach. "He's never really been a water dog, which is silly when you think of it, 'cuz he's got those webbed feet," Skyy mentioned lazily, slowly lifting and lowering her legs into the water. They both watched the droplets of mountain water fall from her toned legs, back into the vastness they came from. "I guess life do be like that sometimes," Skyy mused looking up at the semi-snow-covered peaks cradling them. "We're given these amazing skills and potential, and yet we don't do shit with all that." Summer cocked her head and peered next to this woman who she had only met, but who she longed to know more about.

Skyy glanced back and tossed her another grin. "It's the pot, don't worry." She drew her attention back up to the wooded mountain side.

"I could literally just live out here. It's so quiet and peaceful," Skyy closed her eyes and continued to bask in the sunlight.

"You wouldn't miss things? Like the internet, or ya know, toilets?" Summer questioned. The giggles found her, and soon she realized the weed had taken over for her as well.

Sky tilted her head and gave Summer a side-eye look. "Girl, the more shit we have, the more complicated things get. Ya the internet and my iPhone are dope and have saved my ass more times than I'd like to admit. But think of all the bullshit technology has caused, too. Places like this," Skyy looked around the pristine scenery, "they're slowly being replaced by the dumb little hunk of metal in all of our pockets. Next generation is sincerely fucked."

Summer's high caused her mind to slowly reflect on Skyy's words. She couldn't help but think back to all the times she'd argue with Harry over texting. His accusations over her 'text-tone,' the miscommunication, the uneasiness and suspicions that he could be talking to another girl. She found herself thinking back to the last restaurant they had visited. "Do people even talk to each other anymore?" Summer had asked Harry while scanning the dining room, noting the majority of couples and families who were all nose-deep into their phones or tablets.

"Huh?" Harry had responded, not even glancing up from the glowing machine that held him fixated.

"Seriously?" She scowled at him from across the table.

"What? Come on babe, you know it's playoffs!"

"Sure, but I picked this place specifically so you wouldn't be watching the game." She should have known better. Harry always seemed to find a way to get what he wanted, leaving Summer unsatisfied and questioning her priorities.

She was guilty of being addicted to her phone as well, but argued that she had a balance to her relationship with it. *It's part of my job. Marketing is literally getting people to pay attention and to get hooked*, she thought, her mind slowly coming back to the log, Skyy, and finally to the empty space that filled this void between two mountainsides.

"Alright, enough philosophical bullshit. I didn't mean to be a buzzkill," Skyy said as she playfully nudged Summer in the shoulder, snapping Summer fully back to reality.

"Come on. Log meditations are over. I got the munchies! And you look better wet." With that exclamation and another spirited prod, Skyy pushed Summer back off the log and into the water before quickly jumping in after her. Atlas barked frantically at the pair as they swam back to the shore, their laughter and splashing filling more than just empty space between the two mountainsides.

Chapter 6

Skyy had helped Summer set up camp. Her small one-person tent sat just off the waterline, tucked away where the trees met the beach. Their friendliness had evolved quickly, and they lay on their bellies, side by side, propped on their elbows with half of their bodies sticking out of the tent. They faced the twinkling water, tossing multicolored Gusher candies into each other's mouths. Hysterical laughter followed each time one of them missed.

"I haven't had Gushers since I was like, I don't even know, ten?" Summer mused, tossing another of the geometrically shaped morsels into Skyy's open mouth.

"What?! Girl, they're the best! I always keep some on me," Skyy exclaimed. "They got the juice!" she sang out, which was quickly followed by Summer's appreciative wheezing.

"How are you so funny?" Summer beamed, her cheeks red from laughing. Or, perhaps it was because she hadn't realized how very close Skyy's face was to hers.

"And how are you so beautiful?" Skyy shot back, without missing a beat. Skyy's lips stole the rebuttal straight from Summer's mouth as she leaned over and kissed her. It was soft, slow, and tender. Gentle and knowing. Summer tasted Skyy's lips and realized she didn't want it to end. Summer had never kissed another girl before. Now, she guessed she was just like Katy Perry. If all girls kissed like Skyy, she may be finding herself playing for the other team as well.

Skyy leisurely pulled back, leaving just a hint of space between their two faces. "There I go, being forward again," she languidly whispered along with the trickling of water coming up the shore.

Summer merely bit her bottom lip and opened her eyes to find Skyy's bright and vibrant ones seemingly consuming the entirety of her soul.

"Well, better to move forward than backward," Summer said breathlessly as she leaned in this time and kissed Skyy, more forcefully than even she herself had expected. A deep seeded and caged lust bubbled up from her gut, breaking something free within her.

Still propped on their elbows in the tent under the trees, the two kissed. Summer shuddered in thrill as Skyy's tongue explored its way into her mouth. Not over-aggressive (like most men she'd made out with), but definitely purposeful. She answered with a push and flick of her own that sent shivers creeping down her spine. With a careful and smooth maneuver, Skyy rolled Summer onto her back and straddled her. Wasting no time, Skyy leaned forward and began kissing Summer with a newfound hunger. She gently took Summer's bottom lip between her teeth and pulled them back before letting her tongue dance back inside. Their rhythmic and heavy breathing quickly grew between them to a thundering crescendo as they enveloped into each other, words forgotten and replaced with desire to explore and be exposed. Skyy pulled back, gently tugging at Summer's shirt as she pulled their bodies closer. Their faces turned into mirroring dancers as they fell deeper, their bodies seemingly trying to merge into each other. Skyy found the bottom of Summer's shirt and lifted, finding no resistance from either her or the shirt as it gracefully floated up and over her head, then found its way to the floor of the tent. Summer's bra, just as easily, unclasped and fell like a leaf to their sides.

"God, can you teach every man how to do that?" Summer breathed lustily through her tight grin, before laying back down and allowing Skyy to hover over her chest.

"We can't ever tell them our secrets, otherwise they might really think they rule the world," Skyy teased before running just the tip of her tongue over Summer's nipple.

Summer's eyes shut and her jaw opened as she gasped to expel a hot and heavy breath she hadn't realized she'd been holding. Skyy's tongue continued to probe around and around Summer's nipple, and it responded by perking up and hardening until it was like one of the rock faces that surrounded them. Her tongue was a master sculptor, carving the stone before it, creating beauty and truth from Summer's body. A hand found Summer's opposite breast and put itself to work, cupping and caressing the mound beneath it lovingly while Skyy's tongue adjusted and took on the pattern of a figure skater, skating across her skin. As if carefully choreographed, Skyy's mouth hovered over the other nipple, but she left her hand there to cup it, knead it, and bring it closer to her face as she repeated her performance.

"Fuck," Summer whispered, her nails digging into the slippery fabric as she tightly clutched the sleeping bag under her with both hands while Skyy worshipped her chest. Teeth found their way to lightly clamp around Summer's nipple, gently pulling the simultaneously soft and hard flesh back before letting go. Summer stared through her long lashes to find Skyy moving downward, her gentle mouth kissing the skin just under her chest. Skyy's eyes returned a burning look back at her as Summer watched this woman she just met slowly drag her lips down, down, down her stomach until they were brushing the hem of her shorts.

"You're a goddess, you know that right?" Skyy purred, her smoldering eyes never leaving Summer's as she expertly unbuttoned the shorts, planting more soft, deliberate kisses along the curve of her hip, before returning to her lower stomach. Summer felt herself freed from the shorts, but wasn't sure how it happened so quickly. Once they were off, they disappeared in the tangle of fabric at the bottom of the tent, quickly forgotten. Skyy's lips began to drag lazily across the hem of Summer's bright blue boy shorts. Summer's breathing quickened and anticipation gripped her chest as she realized what was next. To be sure, she lifted her head slightly and watched Skyy's kiss turn into soft nibbles, until eventually clamping down on the elastic fabric at the top of her underwear. Unhurriedly, Skyy dragged the last of Summer's remaining clothing off with her teeth, exposing the soft, shaved pinkness previously hidden underneath.

"Goddess," Skyy whispered again, her eyes igniting with flames as she looked at Summer's pussy like it was an oasis in the Sahara Desert. Skyy lowered her lips until they were hovering just over Summer's glistening mound. Summer arched her back slight in anticipation, knowing what was to come. But Skyy wasn't just going to give Summer what she clearly desired. Instead, she toyed with Summer, like a cat ruthlessly plays with its meal before devouring it.

"This is the sexiest, little pussy I have ever seen." Skyy's voice was just barely audible, even in the silence of the forest. She purposefully breathed hot air across the folds of Summer's labia. Summer never knew air could be so seductive and inviting. She reached, grasping her chest in an effort to slow her labored breathing as Skyy's honeyed breath rolled over her in a wave that crashed over her entire body.

A soft, probing kiss found its way to the curvature between her legs. It was rapidly followed by another. And another. A faint cry escaped Summer's whimpering mouth as Skyy's practiced tongued danced slowly and her throat exhaled with pent up fervor, slipping forcefully in between the wet crack and rolling, rolling, rolling up and around with a purposeful flick before finally hitting her clit.

Again, it slipped in between Summer's crevice before leisurely rolling itself up to her furled fiddlehead. The wave that was her hitched breath had the telltale signs of a tsunami slowly forming. Skyy slithered deeper and deeper into Summer each time she drew her long tongue back from Summer's clit, only to start the motion all over again. The wetness began to spill from her legs, soaking the sleeping bag beneath her and aiding Skyy with lubrication. Summer could hear the soft slurping noise from Skyy and feel the suction with each strengthening wave. Summer's head began spinning, her body quivering each time the tongue rolled and flicked across her hood. Faster, and faster it worked with a precision Summer had never experienced. Skyy was a trailblazer, knowing exactly where to find even the smallest of Salmon berries. Summer's body seized in anticipation of the next wave, ready for it to crash over her and send her spinning and swimming in eternal bliss. When it didn't come, she fluttered her eyes open and peered down her body, only to find Skyy grinning mischievously.

"Are you ready?" Skyy said slyly, while continuing to place soft kisses on the wetness, her eyes never breaking contact with Summer's.

Summer's already knotted brows deepened from confusion as she looked down at Skyy's slick lips.

"Ready? Ready for what?"

Skyy dragged the tip of her tongue vertically along Summer's lips with a grin.

"Ready to experience something more beautiful than this place?" With an expert hand, Skyy laid her palm on Summer's navel. Using her thumb, she applied pressure enough to pull back the hood covering

Summer's throbbing gem. The moment the small nub came into view, Skyy's mouth was wrapped around it. Summer arched and moaned as Skyy's tongue began working in circles around her clit. Around one way, then slowly shifting to go the opposite direction, applying more and more pressure as she did so.

"Oh my god!" Summer covered her mouth in fear of disrupting nature's peace with her whimpering moans. Skyy's tongue expertly hugged Summer's pink flesh as she worked it around and around, never slowing. Then came the next sensation to an already overwhelming experience and Summer cried out sharply as Skyy slowly slid the digits of her middle and index finger of her free hand into the drenched void. Skyy rotated her fingers, so they curled up, finding the spot from inside, massaging it with womanly knowledge.

Summer's body convulsed and writhed as the combination of Skyy's oral muscle wriggling in circles, and the fingers, hooked and digging, brought her to unadulterated euphoria. Skyy played her fingers like a musician, strumming her fingers in and out of Summer to the rhythm of her whirling tongue dancing at the top of Pussy's Peak.

Skyy pulled her face up briefly, slurping as she did, her fingers continuing to thrust, until those too stopped moving. She maintained pressure, her two fingers hooked knuckle deep as Summer's legs contracted and kicked out, her own hand still clamped tightly over her mouth, in an attempt to muffle her moans. Skyy's face bent down again, wrapping her lips around Summer's clit once more. This time, it wasn't fanciful circles and twirls that she conducted; it was rapid flickering of her tongue, left to right, over Summer's stimulated and throbbing skittle. Each time Skyy's tongue flicked over, it pushed just slightly, applying the perfect amount of pressure.

With her eyes closed tightly, Summer saw stars and blackness. It didn't take much time for her to reach the orgasm she knew was coming as Skyy relentlessly strummed over her.

"Okay, okay!" Summer gasped, taking her hand away from her mouth finally and looking down at Skyy as she worked. "Fuck!" Summer squealed, her body arching up as the sensation shot through her body as if being electrocuted. Her entire body was tingling and buzzing as she let herself go and felt the rush of dopamine take over.

Skyy felt it first. The warm release of cum flooding over the two digits she still held taunt and curved inside Summer. She watched gleefully as Summer's juices flowed down her fingers and into her palm. Summer's rigid, and bowed body collapsed, and she heaved with deep unsteady breaths. Her body was trembling, and she let out the smallest of laughs as she touched her hand to her forehead in sheer disbelief of what had just transpired.

Skyy slyly smirked and slowly slid her glistening hand from between Summer's still pulsing gap. When Summer was finally able to open her eyes, they were filled with new light. Skyy winked and wrapped her mouth around her two sticky fingers.

Summer's eyes bulged a little at the kinky action, and shook her head, mesmerized.

"You...oh my god, I don't even know what to say," Summer stammered, biting her lip.

Skyy curled up next to Summer, running a finger up her soft body.

"I told you," she whispered, kissing Summer's ear. "Gushers are my favorite candy."

The two entangled bodies dozed languidly in the summer afternoon heat. Only when they were roused by Atlas' frantic barking did they wake up from their sleepy embrace.

"Atlas," Skyy called, shifting away from Summer and out of the tent. "What is it boy?"

Summer rolled up, tossing her shirt and shorts back on before joining Skyy outside the tent. Loud, boisterous laughter, mingled with Atlas' barks, met

Summer as they reached the shore. The frat boys Skyy previously had encountered at the trailhead were floating in a yellow blowup raft that was making its way lazily down the water until it was perpendicular to the girls and barking Atlas. Muffled music from a speaker mixed with the dog's woofs as the boys lifted their sunglasses to inspect the two beauties on the beach.

"Ayyy!" one of the boys cat-called, whistling. "What's good, girls? You two trying to go for a ride?" The two others in the raft laughed and lifted their cans of cheap shitty gas station beer.

Hands on her hips, Skyy rolled her eyes with impatience. "Ya, no thanks, we're good," Skyy replied condescendingly. "We came out here to be with nature, and ya'll are disturbing the peace, and my patience."

"Aw come on girls, no need to be shy. We know you wanna have a yacht dance party. Come on, plenty of room on this fine vessel to twerk!" The loudmouth turned up the volume so the bass bellowed from the small raft.

"Bye," Skyy sarcastically waved. "Atlas, come," she called to the Newfoundland as she turned and headed back towards Summer's camp.

Summer hesitated for a moment before following. Watching the gyrating boys as they played their shitty music and drank their shitty beer, all made her think of Harry. *This is just how'd he'd act if I'd brought him here*. She found herself thinking how glad she was that he hadn't come. She knew if she had, he would only have tarnished the memories she held onto of her father taking her here, to spend time, just the two of them.

The cocky cat-caller hollered one last time, his grating voice breaking Summer's thoughts

"If you change your mind and need a lil' extra *nature*, we're up just a bit away. Come check out the love tent if you get thirsty."

Skyy dug through her backpack, inspecting her belongings, and making sure she had everything before zipping it closed and slinging it on her back.

"I wish I could stay." Summer knew by the downturn of Skyy's mouth that she meant it. "My brother will be worried if I don't show up by tomorrow. Are you gonna be okay out here?" Skyy swiveled her gaze towards the water where the *S.S. Douchebag* had been just moments before.

Summer forced a smile, shaking her head. She knew this was a spur-of-a-moment thing, and great things like this don't last forever. Fairytales were for younger, desperate girls who still had a father.

"I'll be fine. I got my bear, and boy mace," Summer half-heartedly laughed, tilting her head towards the orange spray can she had fished out of her bag the moment she was back at the tent and away from the frat guys.

"Alight, well, just please be careful." Skyy embraced Summer in a tight hug, then kissed her softly on the lips. "Maybe we'll bump into each other someday. On another trail. Atlas! Come!" With that declaration and a wink, Skyy and Atlas trotted away.

Chapter 7

Darkness found Summer zipped tight and warm in her sleeping bag as she lay on the floor of her tent. The outer rain-cover and windfly was peeled off so she could better experience the night sky, something her father always suggested doing, in spite of how the cold of the mountains airs crept in. Through the mesh screen and the outline of dark tree branches that appeared to be reaching for her, Summer viewed a breathtaking scenery that many would never experience. Out here, without the city lights to pollute the expansive night sky, space opened itself up to Summer and continued beyond. A kaleidoscope of colors washed over her: milky whites bathed with shy purples, dashing blues danced with the ever-flickering light from stars as if reaching out to hold Summer in their twinkling embrace. The edible had long since worn off, but Summer was still riding the high of her experience with Skyy. As her eyes searched and contemplated the juxtaposition of darkness and light from the reaches of space beyond herself, she thought of Skyy's touch, and how small they must have looked from so far away. Were they perhaps a twinkle or glow to some other far-off planet?

Her hand unconsciously meandered down her soft stomach and dug under her shorts. She wasn't surprised to find herself already damp. The mixture of emotions from both her memories of her tryst with Skyy, and the sheer magnitude of the vast space above flooded her with a desperate longing to capture that moment again.

Summer pressed against the small nub that Skyy had found so easily hours before. With two fingers locked closely together, she pressed onto herself and mimicked the same swirling and circling motions that had been Skyy's tongue on her clit. Despite the instant pleasure she brought to herself, Summer kept her eyes wide open, taking in everything before her. Space and stars and the nothingness that was everything holding Earth in orbit overcame her as the fingers quickened in speed. Small semi-circles soon became the very orbital trajectory that clasped this giant rock at the Sun's discretion. Faint, gentle pressure applied to her body soon became the very gravity itself that pinned Summer down on that same foundation. Yet the more pressure Summer applied, the more she felt her body floating away. Soft moans began to leave her mouth as she was leaving the Earth and her corporeal body behind. She was no longer reaching for her orgasm or her encounter with Skyy, but was reaching within herself, desperately trying to free herself with the release of an impending supernova. As Summer explored her own person, caught up and lost in the experience, she was unaware that the heavens and silence that surrounded her were not her only audience.

Ominous whispers from outside the tent snapped her from continuing her own transcendence. Summer jerked upright, listening to the darkness. More murmurs, and the sound of footsteps prodding against the forest floor froze Summer in place as she realized how terribly and utterly alone she was.

"Yo, it's over here," she heard a voice from outside the tent state in a low tone, this time much closer than previously.

"There it is," eagerness oozed out of the whisper. A frightening, deviant and feverish excitement told Summer exactly who was stalking her. *Those fucking frat guys!*

Summer frantically groped around in the darkness, heart pounding, her fight or flight response recognizing that fleeing the tent would only put her directly in their path. *Shit!* She swore she had stashed her mace under her inflatable pillow, but searching in the dark as quickly and quietly as she could resulted in her finding nothing but the cold tarp of the tent floor.

Complete silence caused Summer to stop probing the darkness and she froze, listening once again.

Without warning, the sound of her tent's door frame unzipping sounded, loud as thunder slashing across the sky. The lightweight door hung, loose and limp to the side as the image of three dark figures emerged.

"Having fun with nature yet?" The voice of the cat-caller from the raft earlier chuckled, and before Summer had time to react, two pairs of hands seized her sleeping bag and yanked her from the tent onto the dry, pine covered forest floor.

"Told you we were gonna have a party," the voice hissed. "I'm just a little upset you didn't accept our invite, although we're still gonna have a great time."

The sleeping bag was wrenched out from under Summer, leaving her exposed to the cold ground and these assholes as she scrambled to get to her feet. A pair of hands found her arms before she could stand, pinning her onto the dirt and pine. The smell of alcohol molested her nostrils as Summer opened her mouth to scream. A sweaty palm found its way over her mouth, forcing what was, meant to be a desperate cry into a dull, muffled yelp.

"Bro, I fucking told you to cover her mouth first."

"Dude, shut the fuck up or do it yourself. Where's that other bitch? There was two of them."

"She's not in here. She got some booze though." Summer could hear the clink of fingernails on metal as the figure must have found her father's flask. "Shit's full of sand or something," he exclaimed, tossing it aside with a small thud.

Summer seized her opportunity while the other two lurking figures searched for someone who wasn't there. Biting down on the palm covering her mouth resulted in a sharp yowl from behind her. The palm loosened slightly, and Summer threw her head back, making contact with what she assumed and hoped was a face.

"Fuck!" The voice behind her growled. The moment both hands left Summer, she recoiled back again. This time, the back of her head connected with something solid, but it wasn't a face. The shadow who had been holding her had dropped to the side, leaving Summer's head in direct line with a large rock protruding from the earth. Her head made contact with it, and in the darkness, she saw flashes of bright white as the pain seared through her skull, down her neck and the rest of her body. Feeling as if she was on a boat at rough seas, Summer groaned and attempted to sway herself up onto her hands and knees. She was nearly successful, but before she could get upright, another pair of hands found her ankles and began to drag her through the brush towards the water's shores. Summer twisted and turned, trying to escape the clutches of the invaders hauling her through the undergrowth.

"Help!" she screamed, clawing her hands around her, desperate for anything to grasp onto. She only succeeded in thoroughly scratching all along her arms and palms as the men pulled her further down until she felt the unmistakable soft mixture of gravel and sand of the beach beneath her writhing back.

"Help!" Summer screamed again, her shout echoing across the water as she became hysterical, tears streaming from her eyes. "Someone help!" She was able to cry out once more before another hand, just as grimy and sweaty as the first covered her mouth.

"The fuck! She's gonna wake the whole fucking mountain up. Shut her the fuck up!" It was the loud mouth again, his voice desperate with a sharp hoarseness.

"Time for lights out," the voice covering her mouth taunted from above, his palm moving to cover Summer's nostrils. "Guess you didn't read the trailhead sign--quiet hours start at dusk."

A deafening roar ripped through the mocking laughter above Summer, silencing all three men instantly.

Gooseflesh rose up Summer's skin as the echo of the blast reverberated against the mountainsides across the water before finally fading.

"The fuck was that?" Fear gripped the voice as it spoke out nervously. Summer could only just barely make out the outline of the attacker above her and the two standing at her feet in the faint half-moonlight, but knew they were sharing her unmistakable sense of foreboding.

Just as quickly as the roar had erupted, loud pounding footsteps could be heard rushing towards the space they occupied, followed by a guttural growl so low it sent Summer's heart plummeting into her gut.

"Wh-what the fuck is that?!" Clammy hands released Summer, and she dropped with a thud on the gravelly sand as the outline of a monstrous entity emerged from the green veil behind her. The fraternity boy above her was knocked clear off his feet, accompanied by a sound like that of a large tree branch snapping as he landed with a thud into the thick bushes. Summer watched in horror as the gigantic silhouette of a creature, standing on two legs, easily stepped over her frame as it moved towards the two cowards flinching back towards the water. "Hey man we were just," the quivering, pleading voice of loud-mouth was cut short as Summer watched the shadow being swing its massive arms in a wide arc, sending the two boys flying to the side with the same sickly crack. In the dim light offered by the moon peeking behind a ridge, Summer could see the creature's shoulders heaving rapidly, the hot air of breath rising from its raspy breathing.

"Get up! Get up and run!" The frantic voice pleaded helplessly as he pulled his frat brother to his feet. Summer watched the outline of the two boys drag themselves up and back into the ticket of the forest, leaving her alone on the ground, looking up at the backside of this monstrous creature.

Summer laid frozen, her heart pounding in her ears, as the shadow turned slowly to face her.

The voyeur moon revealed itself fully from the ridge it had been shying under. Moonlight spilled down the mountainside, flooded across the water, and illuminated the beast fully for the first time. Summer's mouth gaped open in horror, like a fish out of water, but no sound emitted.

Towering before her, taller than any man she had ever met, was a being that resembled an erect ape with human features. The rays of moonbeams shone on its toned and rippling abdomen and pectoral muscles, clearly defined even under the mat of dark hair. Arms, the size of thick tree branches hung loosely at its side before it slowly began to raise them wide, pleading almost, as if to embrace Summer.

"Summer," it spoke out, softly, in a low-deep growl that reverberated through Summer's body as she forced herself to look up at its large head. The moon dared not cast light on its face, but the wide jaw and gleaming white teeth were unmistakable, even in the shadow.

"Summer," it repeated, taking a large step towards her, its arms still outstretched.

Summer's head spun, from the knock on the rock or the disbelief of what she saw before her, she wasn't sure.

"No, please," Summer squeaked trying to crawl backwards from the beast. "Please," she whispered, trying to regain control of her body. But as the beast stepped closer and closer towards Summer, her vision began to fade, the pain in her head overwhelming her until the last thing she saw was the creature's large, broad face leaning down over hers.

Through a wave of unconsciousness Summer feels herself being carried in massively strong and furry arms. She peers up to see a face. More ape than human. There is determination, and kindness in its eyes as it marches along. She blames it on her blurred vision. Nothing this monstrous could be kind. The figure that has haunted her nightmares and cast its long shadows from the campfire as her father told her stories...This elusive being could only be whisking her away to consume her body and flesh. She closes her eyes to the terror before her as she loses consciousness again.

Chapter 8

A blurred space filled Summer's vision when she finally awoke. Fluttering eyelashes clapped in unison with the throbbing in the back of her head. She reached back to touch the spot where the rock had met her skull and found her arms in pain as well. Red scratches and dried blood that branched from her arms reminded her of the encounter with the fraternity boys under the moon. But that wasn't all; there was more. There was, *something*. A creature. A giant being.

Realization hit her. No, not just something…Sasquatch.

Summer closed her eyes tightly, holding herself as she pushed the images of the fierce beast aside. *It couldn't have been real. Bigfoot is not real…It was a dream. A bad dream that crept into my mind from the silly stories of my dad.* Her reassurances to herself were in vain as she batted her eyes open more and took in her surroundings.

She was no longer in her tent, nor on the gravelly beach. Instead, she found herself in what appeared to be a bed of soft, dried moss and twigs. No, it wasn't really a bed, she thought. Not a bed, but a nest of sorts. Comfortable enough despite the animalistic feel to it. Before her, a small fire crackled and cast soft shadows on the walls of a small cave that was otherwise bathed in darkness. Along the rocky cave wall were an assortment of items: dried plants, fungi, and fish hung from braided bark, small pots, and pans that she quickly identified as backpacking utensils made to be quickly broken down and stuffed into packs were stacked neatly onto one another. However, the most peculiar items in the eclectic collection were a row of tattered books, all organized by height. She scanned their titles and authors: Carl Jung, Chogyam Trungpa, Shakespeare, Lola Faust, Stephen King, Elizabeth Wilkerson, and Aldous Huxley among them. There were books on engineering, astrology, poetry, and dictionaries in several languages. In her peripheral, the cave's wide opening led way to a veil of gray; a summer rain cloud had found itself chancing upon the area, and was drizzling a steady stream of rain with a softness Summer found soothing to her cranium.

Summer snapped back to focus from the rain's alluring sound and began searching the dim cave for the creature she had encountered. The creature that had no doubt brought her here.

Suddenly, the large shape she had initially and erroneously mistaken for a boulder near the entrance of the cave, stirred. It rose from its cross-legged position and filled the cave's mouth, casting a long, wide shadow across the moss bed Summer awoke upon.

"Summer's heat brings the beauty we see before us, but without water, the sun would see this forest scorched to ash. It is this balance of harmony they share with one another that makes all before us possible." The same deep, low voice that had uttered her name before spoke, turned to face her with a small grin that looked peculiar on a countenance that also reflected a gaze of the deepest concern. Summer stared into the visage she had previously attempted to convince herself was just a dream, a figment of her imagination. The large furry face with its massive jaw and wide nostrils stared back at her. The firelight flickered across its face revealing eyes the color of deepest amber—tree sap, freshly bled from the trunk, weary and weeping.

"It was not my intention to frighten you," the creature spoke, his words calculated and measured, slow in pace, as if contemplating the correct way to articulate them. The cave was just high enough to allow the creature not to stoop as it made its way calmly to the fire, arms wide, proffering the same gesture before on the beach.

"It is not my purpose to interfere with man's doing. I was unable to control myself and I felt compelled to help you, Summer." It sat cross-legged once more across from her. Its eyes, appearing so soft and kind and void of malice in the firelight, offered an apology: "You must have questions," they spoke.

Summer could only stare back in disbelief for several moments, gaping at the great being before her that spoke so gently and with such a pleasant cadence, before she found the courage to form her own words.

She shook her head, as if trying to rouse herself from the dream she kept telling herself she must be in. "How, how do you know my name?" It was a whisper when it finally emerged. "How can you talk?" Her voice grew with confidence, taking it all in. "How are you even real? I mean, Sasquatch isn't real. It's a myth. *You're* a myth. A story. A funny joke on a postcard....." Summer cast her mind back to a memory of the refrigerator in her apartment. Cluttered with photos, receipts, and sticky notes was a lone postcard, the last her father had ever sent her. On it, a cartoon drawing of a Sasquatch sat on a tree stump, head tilted back as it drank from a bronze beer bottle. On the back, her father had scribbled, *Believe*. Guilt flooded her momentarily. Perhaps this was a dream. Perhaps she had died on that beach, either from the knock to her head or by the hands of those predators that had come for her in the darkness. Perhaps this was the heaven invented by her father's stories.

The creature sighed and looked down, almost in shame.

"I have caused you grief. This, among many other reasons, is why I do not present my being to Man." It turned to look toward the slowing rain outside the cave. "My kind would not be pleased to learn that I have brought you here. That we are having this communion of language," a soft chuckle followed before he landed his amber gaze back on her own.

"Summer, the season that marks the sun's utmost rejoice, and its longest station in the sky. A period of our world's finest development, perfection, and beauty. Much like yourself. I can see why Man named you after such a splendid embrace of the Great Star and our world." Heat crept up Summer's face, replacing the burning in her skull if for only a moment.

"I have known you since you were very small," the creature admitted, staring guiltily at the fire before it. "It was your father's stories in the night around a fire that caught my attention when I would stray too close. It was your innocence, laughter, and smell of lilac entwined with wildflower honey that caused me to linger and remain, even when danger told me it was foolish. I do not experience sorrow in the way in which Man does, but the feeling I experienced when you and your father left the forest can only be described as emptiness. It was the first time in my existence that I truly wanted something for myself. An egocentric idea. A human idea. I've ruminated on this conflict within myself for many seasons." Another sigh, followed by that soft and self-deprecating chuckle.

"I have come to acknowledge that those who wander this deep into the forest are not necessarily lost, but feel a deeper connection and appreciation to life than most. Your father was one of them. He showed me, what I can only imagine to be love, through his interactions with you. It was this gift he gave to you, this love, that I found you to blossom before my eyes upon each trip that brought you two here. Your growing curiosity, your justified fears, your inner self finding its true place in the world. There, I found something beyond the simple idea of beauty. I found myself regaining the notation that life had more meaning than my lonely existence.

"I thought," it paused, calculating again as it stared back into the fire. "I thought, I had rid myself of such selfishness when you and your father ceased to return to the forest. I do not usually stay in one place for too long as there are many who wish me harm. Hunters who seek me and my kind for their own gain. I, self-serving and self-absorbed, stayed here longer than I should have, in vain, with the desperate hope that you may one day return."

The hammering in Summer's skull was dulling to the words spoken by this creature. Confusion, mixed with conflicting shame, overcame her as she reflected on the being's predicament.

"I was preparing to leave, as I have caught scent of the ones that would cause me harm in close proximity for some time. But then, I sensed a new aroma. Yours. I had to risk seeing if it was indeed you who had wandered back into this forest. If not, but for a single fleeting instance to glimpse upon you once again."

In all Summer's years, no one had ever spoken of her in such a way. Her face deceived her and blossomed a reddish hue not even the fire could replicate.

"Th-thank you?" Summer managed to stammer out, the conflicting feeling of fear ebbing out of her. Her eyes involuntarily cast downward, as if embarrassed to make eye contact with the creature who spoke such kindness.

"But, so that means you've been watching me? That's a little bit stalkerish, don't you think?" Summer blurted out, regaining some of her mental faculties as her position in the situation became more clear. "And, what the hell, how can you talk?"

A true smile flashed over his face, revealing what Summer thought could be considered almost charming.

"It is my nature to stalk, as you say." That smile again. The Sasquatch contemplated the fire, as if searching for something lost.

"As for my language, my kind first learned to produce sounds that humans understood when we once lived with the People. Before the White Man arrived, my kind and the people lived in harmony. We helped one another exist. We witnessed the coming of White Men and the destruction they brought with them. Wendigos, the People called them. Creatures of greed and gluttony. They stole, and slaughtered, and drove the People away from the forest. We were outnumbered and learned that we could not exist with them like we had with the People. Language, as you know it, was no longer needed as my kind resided into the deepest hollows of the forest where the only language we spoke was silence. It is the only language that brings us safety and secures our kind. Stalker language. It is a language of loneliness."

He spoke to the fire, his eyes lost in its glowing embers. Summer watched him, realizing just how ancient this creature must be. How much he must have witnessed over the course of centuries. Summer felt her chest tighten, imagining the loss he must have endured. Immortality, Summer reflected, was such a vain concept, when one realizes its cost. For every ounce of knowledge that is gained, an amount of humanity is lost.

He was brought back from his thoughtful silence with a crack and spark of the flames.

"I have been alone for many seasons. It is easier to hide and be unseen when you are alone.

There came a day, however, when one became two. This was before I encountered you and your father.

I was, as you say, *stalking*," he chuckled, throwing her a quick smile, "when in the forest, I saw a man, falling from the sky. The wings which allowed him to float down had become tangled in the branches of a tree. I watched him struggle and cry for help." His thick brows knitted as he recalled the interaction.

"It's not our way, but I felt the need to help him. I did not know the language we speak now, so our first encounter was...awkward?" He looked up at Summer as if asking if his diction was correct.

"We found that words were not needed, for us both to be understood. After I had helped free him from his trap, I tried to escape him, but always found him, following me. He was unlike any man I had ever encountered. He had nothing but his wings and that sack, over there, filled with firestarter." Sasquatch nodded towards a dull faded bag along the side of the cave wall. Summer leaned to peer over, inspecting the half-deflated bag, catching sight of what looked like a significant amount of money inside.

"This man, I learned, could not return to the world from which he came from. So I accepted him, as he accepted me. While the seasons passed, he taught me to speak his language; this language we speak now. We traveled often. When we strayed close to the human world, he would slip away, and return with books for me." Sasquatch again nodded to the neat row of books along the cave wall.

"He taught me how to read. He showed me the beauty of language, and, although our time together was short, he was able to teach me some writing." The Sasquatch glanced up at the cave wall above Summer. Summer followed his gaze and saw, in black charcoal a neatly sketched name: D. B. Cooper.

"He was called Cooper. He was the first man, other than the People, who showed me that man can be kind, and trusted, and," Sasquatch's lips fumbled to find the right words, "possibly, the first man to show me that friendship could exist between our two worlds. It is because of him that that I have found the courage to speak to you."

Sasquatch stared at Summer with a fierceness that left her afraid, but also with a vague sense of endearment towards the beast.

The chuckle, now a comforting sound to Summer's ears, broke their trance. "For a being that couldn't speak human, I seem to have a lot to say." He beamed at her and in his smile, Summer found him irresistibly majestic, fur, and all.

Summer's mind raced with emotions, and more questions. *D. B. Cooper. A bag full of money. A man who fell from the sky? Why does this all sound so familiar?* Summer reached into the recesses of her memories, knowing this name and story sounded of a legend she had learned of when she was younger. But here in the cave, her thoughts kept pushing towards

Sasquatch. A push that put Summer into the acceptance of his being.

"Did I answer all of your questions?" He asked, studying her.

Summer fumbled: "Yes. Well, no," she laughed, a comfortability forming between them. "I mean, I have like, a million more questions but, I'm not sure how important they really are now."

She scanned the cave over once more. "Where is Cooper now?"

Sasquatch looked out towards the mouth of the cave. The rain had stopped, and summer's blue sky-smile was showing its teeth through the hazy clouds.

"He suffered from his journey through the sky and our travels. It was too much for him. I gave him back to the Earth, just before seeing your father for the first time. Your father came to the forest first as a young boy, as I'm sure you know."

Summer knew her father had been infatuated with the outdoors since childhood. But the realization that this creature had been so close to her and her father, for so long, made Summer feel a connection. It shared with her, in some ways, memories of her father-- memories she could not share or express with others. Two creatures, so drastically different, were nothing more than specks of space, orbiting each other. The pull of gravity reaching its full force at this very moment, where they had collided into one another.

The throb in Summer's skull brought her firmly back to Earth. She winced as she lightly prodded the now fully formed bruise.

"You suffer," Sasquatch noted, matter-of-factly.

Summer nodded, still contemplating if the bump from her head was the cause of this dream-like scenario.

The creature stood, his massive body towering over Summer, making her feel small.

"I can take you to a place where you may be healed. If you'll let me?" He reached out a giant gray palm, its fingers the size of small bananas.

Summer studied the enormous palm before laying her own small one in his.

"Okay," she said, looking up at him. "But, first, one last question." She asked with a shy smile.

"One answer. A short one this time. I promise," he flashed his charming smile and gently closed his hand around her, enveloping it completely.

"What do I call you? Do you have a name?"

He easily pulled her up so the two stood close, his smile shining down on her.

"For now, you can call me friend."

Chapter 9

The pair traversed through the woods. Summer was amazed that such a giant creature could walk so quietly as he led the way before them. She watched as his, well, big feet, trended with knowing, never landing on any living thing, as if on purpose.

"Ok, but like, what about a real name?" Summer found herself playful now that they were out of the dark cave. The summer rainstorm had passed, leaving the forest damp and lush with the aroma of dank earth baking under the sun. *Petrichor*. Her father had always stated that it was his favorite smell.

He peered back at her, sharing her playfulness, noting her beauty as the sun crept through the branches above them.

"Humans love to label, don't they?" He chuckled, turning to lend his palm once more to help her over a fallen tree that was blanketed in moss and fungi.

Summer grinned, allowing his chivalrous actions to help her cross the log.

"It helps us understand," was the only rebuttal she had to advocate for her species.

"Does it?" He gently pulled her up onto the log. The sturdy trunk gave her a height advantage, and she found herself looking directly into his eyes. Their faces were close, closer than they had ever been before, and she caught herself gazing into the amber depths before stepping back down onto the wet forest floor.

"There are four-hundred and thirty different definitions for the English word 'set'," he responded while leading the way again.

"What? No way!" Summer was caught off guard but laughed at what she knew was the sheer ridiculousness of the English language.

"Three-hundred and sixty-eight for the word 'go'." The forest gave way to a slight decline. Through the trees Summer spotted the shimmer of water.

"Okay, fine, Professor Bigfoot," Summer jokingly sang.

He spun around with such quickness Summer nearly ran into him. His brows furrowed together as he stared down at her. Swift terror suddenly flooded her body as she looked up at his fierce face.

"That, is highly offensive." He breathed down on her. They stood in the silence of the forest, Summer trembling with uncertainty and fear. Then with the same abruptness, Sasquatch leaned his head back and gave a deep throaty laughed.

"I apologize. I'm still working on my humor." He gave her an exaggerated wink, before resuming his leisurely ramble down the trail once more. "Cooper was very fond of humor," he mused.

"Okay then, Mr. Sassy" she giggled, giving his lower back a playful push. As her hand laid upon his body she was overwhelmed with how soft his thick fur felt through her fingers.

Sasquatch chuckled. "What's in a name? That which we call a rose, by any other word would smell as sweet," he quipped, reciting one of Summer's favorite lines from Shakespeare. "Okay, let's give me a name, shall we?"

The sunlight reflecting off of the water between the trees grew closer, and with it, the faint sound of rushing water.

"Well, Harry would be fitting, but that's my ex-boyfriend's name."

"Ex-boyfriend?" He echoed. "As in, a mate?"

Summer laughed. "Yeah, I guess mate would be the right word. Have you ever had a mate?" she asked curiously, having never thought of this until now.

"Yes. Just one." He left the words hanging in the warm pine-filled air. "But that was many seasons ago."

Summer felt as if she had struck a chord with him and pushed on, with a flash of something that felt similar to jealousy bubbling inside her.

"Okay, name, name, name. I know. What is your favorite thing in this forest?"

Sasquatch turned to regard her. "Favorite?"

"Yeah. You know, like, what's the one thing out here that you love the most?"

"I'm not sure I feel love the way humans do. I appreciate all the forest has to offer." Sasquatch turned his head to survey the area around them. "Unlike humans, the forest and I share a reciprocal relationship. I take only what I need, and always give back. Humans are the only beings on this Earth that do not give that which they take."

Summer thought about his statement as the trees began to space further apart and the soft hum of water turned into the unmistakable soft surge of a waterfall.

Sasquatch felt her silence and stopped as they reached the gravelly shore of a small pool of water, nestled up against a high rocky cliff that rose to meet a small, bubbling waterfall cascading over its edge and into the pool below.

"Well," he said, taking in the secluded sanctuary. "I suppose if I had to pick, the Cedars are my closest friends. They speak to me the most." He began to make his way towards the steady falls.

"Speak to you?" Summer asked, trailing closely behind him, all the while basking in the experience that was the beauty of this magical place. Small white and yellow wildflowers outlined the pool's edge, while a bright green carpet of moss contrasted starkly up along the cliff's rocky walls just behind the falls.

"Everything speaks, if you choose to listen." Reaching the small waterfall from the side, he dunked his giant hands under, and soaked them under the spray.

"Cedar's a good name," she suggested. She immediately thought of all the young, unfortunate children of millennials who were named Cedar, reflecting on it with an internal cringe. If she had been back home, the name would immediately invoke a feeling of pretension, suitable only for people who lived in the city and ventured into the woods once a summer to get a new profile picture for Instagram. Out here in the wilderness, though, the name felt right.

"Come," he reached his palm out, taking her hand and gently leading her to the side of the cascading water. "I come here when I am hurt. These waters come from the mountains and the sky. They heal you." Summer's obvious hesitation caused him to smile.

"It's quite warm." He stepped into the water, letting it wash over him. He was quickly doused, his pelt turning jet black and slick as he ran his large hands over his face. Summer watched, keenly aware and transfixed as his fur laid into his body, revealing the layers of strong muscles underneath.

Get a grip, she thought, as she shook herself. Disbelief how the sight of such a strange creature could have such an effect on her. Despite herself, she accepted her appreciation of his body under the water, and decided if she was to do this, she would do it the way he felt it. Here, in this secluded space, she felt a primal surge of wanting to be in her natural state.

Her top and sports bra were tossed aside before she found herself wading into the ankle-deep pool. This was so unlike her, she realized, but plunged further into the water, determined. The misty air felt cool on her skin and she shivered while embracing this daring action. Summer had never considered that the Sasquatch was fully naked at all times; the fur coating him completely never lent way to any crudeness she'd find back in the city. Out here, in this secluded space she felt safe enough to peel her shorts off and join him in his state of pure and unadulterated nature. He moved aside to allow her to step under the falls. His eyes, she noticed, were not mindlessly adhered to her perky chest as most men would have, but locked upon her own.

She let the water rain down on her. The pleasant pressure the falls brought her here immediately transported back to her own shower, the one she had right before leaving on this adventure. The water washed over her cuts, the dried blood, and the great bruise on her head, cleansing her. He was right. The waters did find her feeling healed from the pain that had been inflicted upon her the night before.

A wad of wet moss wiped down her arm as he offered to clean her wounds. His free hand stroked her wet hair with grace, trailing his fingers down to her chin, his eyes never leaving hers. She looked up into his great amber eyes and felt herself coming encased in their resin.

"I never did thank you for saving me." She whisper breathlessly, feeling so small beneath his large frame.

He contemplated her for a moment. "I watched you fight back. You very well could have saved yourself." The fingers left her chin and wavered down her neck, tracing her collarbone as one would trace the embedded groves of bark on a tree. "A tree sapling may be small in size, but it does not quit its growth in nature's defiance. Even the grass, though such an insignificant plant to humans, is the strongest structure that grips the Earth, always bending back upright after being prodded on and cut down. The roots grow deep, both in trees and grass. Where one patch falls, a new one always rises to take its place. Stronger as a whole." His massive hand floated over her breast, before pulling back abruptly.

"My apologies," he seemed genuinely embarrassed. "I should have asked." She smiled at his gesture.

"No, I want you to." A feral urge surged through her as she took his hand and led him the few steps it took from the showering falls to the encasement of the rocky ridge that hung over them.

Chapter 10

Summer's hands planted themselves against the spongy wet moss wall that arched under the streaming water. Leaning at an angle, she turned to look back, presenting herself to him as she spread her legs. Her heart raced, threatening to escape her throat as he drew closer. Soft, massive hands found her shoulders as he caressed her down, taking his time, she knew, in his appreciation of all things wondrous. They continued to slowly trail down her side. She was the slope of the forest mountain, and he was the stalker, his fingers slowly encircling her until they clasped tightly around her waist. Instinctually, her back arched, prostrating her round behind at an angle no animal could resist.

She could feel the heat radiating from his groin, encasing her skin with its pheromones as he slowly pressed up against her. The wide, bulbous head of his cock found the wetness between her legs from underneath as it nuzzled into her.

A wave of shock and fear took her momentarily: *fuck, is that even going to fit?* Her fear justified as the shear girth of the mushroom shaped member prodded the crevice between her lips. A line from a famous movie came to mind: *"life, uh…finds a way."*

Summer closed her eyes and accepted his girth. Her lips gave way to this glorious creature as she felt him enter her—white hot pleasure took her where she expected pain and struggle. He filled not only her body, but the loneliness she had felt for so long. A gasp escaped her open mouth as she clung to the moss wall, feeling herself tightening around his thickness as a steady rocking motion began. For such an enormous being, he was gentle as he began to fill her, as if knowing how easily he could rip her in half. Summer's breathing quickened with each pump of his cock as it soon found a steady rhythm. He pushed himself further into her, pulling back until just the head remained, then flowed into her again, giving him more of her each time. Her pussy walls threatened to collapse as he filled her completely, nearly turning her inside out as he pulled back.

A low growl from the creature caused her to flood his cock with her wetness. She could hear the soft gushy sound of her juices covering him with each push, could feel the ease her natural lubrication brought to accommodate his size. It didn't take much for him to completely fill her, feeling the fat juicy head colliding with her cervix wall, the pressure releasing steady moans that blended with the music of the waterfall collapsing into the small pool. His steady rhythm and the wide maw of his cock rubbing into her g-spot was more than enough to cause Summer to arch back and cum. Her body tensed as she came--more quickly than any man she had been with--tilting her head back in ecstasy, all while he never ceased his steady pumping. She looked back at him, trying to catch her breath. She could see the look of concentration and gentleness in his face, but in those eyes, she saw something else. An animal begging to be let free.

"You don't have to be so gentle," she whispered, the sensation of her orgasm still sizzling inside her, waning to push herself further; the fear of what sort of animal she may be unleashing, mixed with a desire to play with fire was overwhelming.

He merely nodded, as if to speak would break the spell that had been cast upon them by the magic of the forest.

He gave no warning.

His fingers tightened around her waist, causing her to lift for a moment, before he began to turn his soft steady rhythm into the pounding of a ceremonial drumbeat. With his first forceful thrust, Summer's face was pushed into the carpeted wall that cushioned her cheek as she cried out. He plowed into her, a caged beast finally breaking free of its chains. Her mind was unable to keep up with the overwhelming sensation that was the constant wet friction he delivered to her, only quickening and deepening with each forceful thrust.

Due to his height, he had to lean back to accommodate the angle of which his cock speared her-- a wall siting position even the most athletic men would collapse from.

But, he was no man.

He was the forest, the trees, the rushing water, and wilderness that had captivated her so long before. The leverage of his muscular thighs only gave him more power, and a seat for Summer to fall back onto as his hips found their full momentum.

His earthly growls gave way to a primitive howl that reverberated off the cliff walls hugging them. The animalistic sound gripped Summer with its primal lust as she cried out with him. His forearm-sized appendage was a force of unrelenting power as he took her completely. Summer's eyes rolled in the back of her head, as what should have been pain from the physical restructuring of her vagina was replaced by an act of nature she could not begin to fathom or explain. He was a raging river, forever roaring through the forest's heart, the erosion that shaped the soft smooth rocks on which he beat against.

He gave a final primal yowl, following the forceful clap that found Summer's ass making full contact with his Sasquatch scrotum. He held her there, his length and girth swelling inside her, threatening to rearrange her organs as she came. Sweet, creamy nectar seeped from her meadow and dripped down onto the earth's grinning face.

Her breath was a thunderstorm of static electricity as she lost herself to time and space. He slowly pulled out of her, dragging with him her glistening womanly sap.

Summer collapsed on the moss wall, its wet fuzziness coating her in its ancient, primordial whispers. *You belong* here, it seemed to speak to her. *This is home*. Her body shuddered as she tried to regain her composure. His soft, gentle palm grazed across her cheek as she turned to face him. His boulder of a chest rose and fell in great heaves. The fire in his eyes was fully stocked with no sign of soon extinguishing.

He leaned down to embrace her, kissing her tenderly before lifting her chin with his fingers. The great humanoid towered over her, his eyes lost to insatiable lust.

"More." His voice, hardly audible through the ceaseless falls behind him, was not his own but replaced by something only the forest could understand. But she knew. At that moment, she understood him completely.

With the ease one has picking up a small pebble, he lifted her by her hips and brought their lips to union once more. They embraced each other passionately as Summer closed her eyes and wished for this moment to never end. She ran her hands through the hair at the nape of his neck, stretching her fingers, tangling them with the thick dark hair, pulling him to her.

Summer felt herself slowly slide down his wetted coat as he lowered her onto himself. Accustomed to his size, she fit around his cock with ease and cried out as he filled her once more. His hands held her in a tight grip as he began lifting her up and down, bouncing her as an otter skitters from rock to rock. Legs and arms wrapped around his powerful body as she held on tightly. His wet fur filled her nose with sweet musk as she buried her face into his hairy chest.

As she clung to him, her cries of overwhelming sensation grew louder and louder as he brought her down on him harder and harder, again and again. The loud wet smack of her juices and the suction of her body being pulled down his entirety filled the air. She could feel herself uncontrollably dripping on him with each pull.

He grunted and snarled now, his pace quickening as she aided in his pull, propelling herself down on him. She felt a wildness overcome her, throwing her head back as he suspended her in the air, his cock acting as her tether to the earth.

"Cedar!" She moaned his new name with the sloshy sound of her orgasm, coating his cock with another gush. Bucking his hips up to meet her throws, he howled as he met her at the same time—throbbing, swelling, his cock erupted inside her, mixing with her own fluids. As he pulsed inside her, Summer felt hot, thick, rope after rope of ejaculation fill her. It didn't take much to overfill her cup and she felt the gush of his cream overflow as it escaped from her depths.

A dam can only hold so much water back and Summer's burst with his final wet thrust and the warming sensation of his fluids coating her inside and out. He held her there, releasing her hips to wrap his large arms around her back. His Sasquatch sized cock remained stiff and throbbing, keeping her upright as he slowly stepped back into the falls.

The water fell gently down upon them. Summer closed her eyes and nestled her exhausted body into his as she felt the warmth wash over them. It was a baptism of union and rebirth as they shared the earth's watery ceremony. An embrace of passion and understanding and a cycle that has come full circle.

She broke from his furry chest to find him gazing down upon her. His eyes had cooled to embers, but still shone with pure desire for her.

"What are you thinking?" She asked, exhausted and dizzy.

He grinned and leaned down to kiss her.

"I was thinking," he said, parting from her lips. "That I have just found my new favorite thing."

They floated their way back along the path which they came. Summer stumbled frequently, still tipsy from the experience and unsteady on her feet. The sticky late-summer heat seeped through the branches, casting a haze on the undergrowth that made her believe this was all but a dream.

"So," she offered to break the silence of the forest. "That definitely wasn't your first time." She smirked playfully as he returned the smile.

"No. As I told you, I had a mate before. One like me. But, you would be my first human." He threw her a devilish grin before snapping his head around, intently scanning the surrounding area.

His tension was immediately palpable.

"What's wrong?"

But, before he could reply, their ears were met with the distinct shattering crack of a rifle firing in the distance. He darted towards the sound before the final echo of the gunshot had even left the forest's ears.

"Cedar! Wait!" She cried after him. She was no match in chasing him, as her short legs couldn't even cover half the distance for his single long gait. He rushed through the brush of foliage, leaving a wake of fluttering ferns. He quickly became only a glimpse of brown and black between the trees as she desperately raced after him.

Summer fought her way through the dense forest before emerging into a small clearing of mountain grass and wildflowers. She clasped her mouth as she saw Cedar kneeling over an enormous stag, slumped and still in the mountain's meadow. He traced its back with one finger delicately as she slowly approached.

"Cedar?" She spoke out to him as she cautiously drew near.

A heavy sigh escaped him.

"This creature was my friend. I have known him since his creation." Cedar spoke, not with sadness, but clarity, void of any emotion. The exchange left Summer feeling confused by the irony of his statement. In that moment, Summer saw her father's death. *Was this how they found him? Fallen on the earth like that of an old worn tree. Lifeless. Alone.* She choked back tears as Cedar tenderly laid the stag's wide alert eyes closed.

Voices crept into the stillness of the clearing. Cedar's head turned in their direction. He swiftly stood, shoulders back and poised. Summer realized in that moment how powerful he was as he opened his massive jaw wide and let loose a threatening roar, its undertone one of melancholy.

The voices, belonging to two hunters approaching the clearing, stopped abruptly and the forest laid still for a moment. Cedar leaned forward, releasing a final howl that beat Summer's ear drums, the silence broken, accompanied by the frantic sounds of frightened footsteps scurrying away back into the forest's depths.

Cedar kneeled once more, resting his palm on the creature's back, speaking in low and rough sounds that Summer could not distinguish.

A sudden rage coursed through her as she bemoaned not just this moment, but that of her father's unexpected death.

"Why did you let them get away with this?" She screamed, pointing in the direction of the diminishing footsteps. "Why did you scare them off! They shot that poor deer! And you just let them go?!" The emotions that had been festering inside her since her father's passing cascaded out of her.

"Summer," he spoke still gazing upon the stag. "Our stories are that of both creation and death. One cannot exist without the other."

His calmness only infuriated her further.

"So, then what was all that talk about giving what we take? They took that deer's life! You should take theirs! Or are you just a hypocrite!"

Cedar turned his gaze to her and offered an apologetic expression tinged with forlorning.

"All life is precious, even if misguided. To kill a wendigo in vengeance would only transform me into the same. All things come to an end. I protect life. I give. I do not take." With his words, the dream Summer had wandered into ended; the fire that fed her father's stories was extinguished.

"I want to go back. Take me back to my tent, *now*!" She spoke with a forced defiance, despite the longing that seemed to catch her throat.

Cedar cast his eyes toward the sky.

"We won't make it by the nights coming. We will rest in my shelter, and I will return you come sunlight." He stood from the stag, regarding it one last time before turning to lead her back into the forest together, but once more alone in their own worlds.

Chapter 11

The two sat sulking in the cave, bathing in the light expelled by the small fire Cedar started. Summer sat slouched in the soft moss nest, her anger slowly melting in the fire's heat. Even though physically they were in close proximity, Summer felt the palpable distance between them. It ate at her core, leaving her feeling childish and slightly ashamed about her earlier outburst.

"I'm sorry," she offered, breaking the silence.

"It wasn't just the deer or those hunters. I lost my dad not too long ago. He was the only family that I had." It was the first time Summer had spoken these words to another being, and she fought to keep her composure, barely able to hold back the tears that were threatening to escape.

"He was my best friend. All of my greatest memories were ones that we created together. He meant so much to me, and in a single moment, he was just gone." She closed her eyes, and a single tear branched its way down her cheek.

"It was an accident while he was working," she explained through trembling lips. "And just like that deer, in an instant, he was gone." Summer thought of the flask back at her campsite and felt guilty for leaving it abandoned. "That's why I came back here. I brought his ashes with me. To take him to our favorite place, one last time." Cedar measured her with a look of compassion and understanding.

"I know we come from two completely different worlds." She spoke to him through bleary eyes.

"I know we see the things differently. You are everything that humans aren't. Back there, with the deer, seeing my dad, it's just hard to accept how cruel life can be. I wish I could accept it all as you do."

She drew her knees into her crest, wrapping her arms around them, cocooning herself in protection. Despite the fire's heat, she shivered gently.

Cedar rose and crept towards her, situating himself next to her in the bed of moss.

"We are different," he agreed, nestling close to her. "Without any fur, you find coldness much more quickly." He teased lightly, encasing her in his giant arms. She accepted his warmth and comfort, burying her face into his hairy chest.

"Life is neither cruel, nor kind." He spoke softly as he pulled her into his lap, stroking her hair with tenderness.

"It does not contemplate or measure. It is merely our experiences that bring you the emotions you are feeling. We do see the world differently, because of those experiences. But once you realize that our time here is nothing more than a cycle of causation and effect, you may free yourself from the human concept of good or bad.

"I know your father's death has brought you pain and sorrow. But it is also his death that has brought you to me." He lifted her chin to face him. "Every ending welcomes a new beginning. Therefore, there is no ending to our story." He kissed her, his large palm cupping her small face.

Summer's mind swam with confusion and conflicting emotion as she kissed him back, allowing herself to cherish this moment. He turned to gently lay her back on the soft moss under them, his lips finding their way to her chin, plummeting off to wet her neck. She felt him breathing her in with his wide nostrils, inhaling her essence. The heat of his breath wafted down her collar bone as she lifted her shirt to him, presenting her perky breasts.

He cupped her chest with his massive hands, pushing them together as he leaned into her, kissing the skin around her erect nipples. She squirmed under him, yearning for his body against her own. He traversed downward with tongue and teeth, stopping for a moment to nibble gently on her flesh until finding his way to the entrance of her cave. He gnawed on the hem of her boy shorts with a growl that expressed his hunger. He gripped her shorts with his massive teeth and one swift jerk pulled back, ripping them off her.

She gasped in shock, yet felt herself moisten in response to the primal behavior. Her torn shorts hung loosely from his oversized teeth. Clutching her chest, Summer spread her legs further for him. As he lowered his face to her, the mangled shorts falling to the side. He opened his mouth and lolled his wide pink tongue across her mound. His oversized tongue filled the entirety of her soft pussy as he laid it upon her, lapping her up like an animal drinks up water.

What he lacked in Skyy's expertise of the woman anatomy, he made up for with his primitive instincts. He scooped her lips up into his mouth as he mowed on her flesh with hunger. He was an animal in heat, drinking her up with an insatiable appetite she had never before experienced. It was as if the perfectly formed space between her legs held sweet nectar, and he was a predator feasting on its caught prey.

Her body writhed and arched uncontrollably as his ravenous tongue dabbed her juices; he slurped and slobbered loudly as he drank her in. A single string of saliva hung from his dark lips as he pulled back momentarily, savoring her flavor. He dove back, driving his tongue between her drenched walls, slithering and whirling his long tongue inside her. She reached down and gripped the thick fur atop his head. Her cries mirrored his rhymical slurping, his tongue continually exploring deeper into her. He massaged her insides with his dexterous primate tongue, it not taking long for her to release herself into his mouth. He grunted in excitement over her juicy flavor, all the while still slurping loudly, while feasting on her cream.

He leaned his face forward, looking up at her. Her cum, mixed with his saliva, dribbled down off his lips onto her throbbing pussy, contributing to the mess of fluid. The thick white goo clung to his furry chin, the contrast not unlike the iridescence of phosphorescent mushrooms standing out in the darkness.

"Cedar," she whispered, closing her eyes and clutching her face as she tried to stop her head from spinning. She felt him crawling over her, his weight shifting the love nest of moss. The heavy, wet slap of his penis smacking against her pussy caused her to look down. Kneeling between her legs, his enormous cock lay on her stomach, the tip reaching well past her belly button. Pushing his hips back, the trunk-like appendage dragged slowly down her belly, massaging her wet and sticky vagina as it passed over its peak. His eyes never left hers and as he pushed his hips forward again, his cock met no resistance, splitting her open as he slid inside. Her mouth gaped open, but no sound was heard. He plunged into her with ease, everything already lubricated and slick. His large, powerful arms steadied themselves near her face as he began to rock into her. The size and sheer force of his Sasquatchhood pressed her back into the nest, threatening to break the twigs and compacting moss. Flexing and grunting, he worked his hips with a rhythmic motion and increasing speed, creating a harmonious wet friction between them. He never allowed his arms to fail him, there was no threat that he'd collapse his massive body onto hers. Instead, he held himself erect and taut, a giant forest tree, sticking out at an angle from the side of a mountain, never bending to the winds' relentless pounding.

"Cedar!" She cried out, her moans echoing off the cave's walls. He replied in his earthly growl, panting as his cock continued its penetrating motion. It was the now familiar pressure of his member, pressing constantly in just the right spot that brought her to completion. Lifting her head up, she watched as the shadows of their entwined bodies, cast from the crackling fire, danced before her. *How similar we are*, she suddenly realized. *Two dark shapes, leaving our mark upon the earth's heart, like hieroglyphs left by its earliest inhabitants.*

Summer felt him tense, and she focused her attention back onto him. He huffed and howled, bucking his hips back, his throbbing cock releasing from the tight grip her pelvic muscles had encased him in. It swung upwards and erupted. An avalanche of thick semen fountained over her, coating her chest and abdomen. Each release brought forth another flash flood of Bigfoot funk. Her naked body glistened in the firelight, and his cock bounced and nodded one last time, expelling his final load onto her pussy, covering it in a glazed frosty layer. He gave a final huff and bent to kiss her, rolling onto his side to admire her spent body.

"Holy fuck," she breathed, trying to slow her breath. She glanced down at the sticky mess that was her body, steam from his seed rose in wisps. She leaned back and laughed in disbelief.

"You, sir, are making it really hard for me to leave in the morning." The warmth of his load slowly seeped down the sides of her inner thighs, coating her like a blanket.

"It would seem that I am perhaps, a hypocrite, as you put it." A low purring throttled from his throat.

"You know I have to leave, don't you?" she mourned, turning to look at his dark face.

He looked down to avoid her eyes.

"I don't belong here. I'm not like you. I don't understand the forest the way you do."

He nodded, understanding the situation.

"Well, then, best to savor the moment. Shall I clean you?" He asked, sitting back up. There was no response from Summer. She was too busy being occupied by his tongue. He had quickly scooped up a mouthful of his warm sass off her stomach, her body trembling with the feeling of electrifying deviance as he pushed it into her mouth and whispered, "Swallow."

Chapter 12

The morning mist and drizzle from another passing summer rain cloud was fitting, as both were quiet, preoccupied with thoughts of their unspoken feelings while they traveled back toward Summer's tent site. He would turn to look back at her periodically, his face stoic and expressionless. She was unsure if he was looking back to check that she was still with him, or if he was trying to capture these last moments with her. By midday, they had found the unique boulder that indicated the trail to Summer and her father's secret spot. Cedar stopped abruptly and looked around the space, flaring his nostrils as he sniffed.

"Everything okay?" Summer asked, worried this may be a gunshot repeat.

"I'll find you at your tent," he spoke before rushing off into the scrubs and trees. Summer watched worriedly as he disappeared in silence. Apprehensively, she trekked on alone to find her tent left in disarray from her encounter with the fraternity of wendigos.

She hunched over, scanning the area until she caught sight of the shiny mental of her father's flask laying near a large protruding tree root.

"Sorry dad," she apologized to the flask, picking it up to inspect it. "I got, well I got a bit distracted."

"Summer!" A familiar voice called from behind her. She turned to find Harry trashing his way through low-hanging branches, fumbling through them like a newborn deer. He was clearly out of his element, his hair disheveled and clothes torn and dirty.

"Harry?" A dumbfounded response left her frozen as she watched him emerge from the trees.

"Summer! I can't believe I found you! I was so fucking worried!" He pressed himself into her, kissing her hard. She pulled back, grimacing from the taste he left on her lips.

"What are you doing here?" she asked, her eyes darting wildly around for Cedar's appearance and the questions that would ensue.

"What do you mean what am I doing here? You were supposed to be back by now. I got worried something had happened to you." For a moment, she found solace in the idea that Harry had actually worked up the gumption to make the journey into the woods to find her. But it wasn't enough to keep her from halting his second attempt to access face, her hand outstretched firmly on his chest.

"Summer, what the hell?" Confusion spread over his face as he regarded her, perturbed by her reaction.

"How did you even find this spot?" She took a step back, distancing herself from him. He matched her steps, grabbing her wrist and pulling her towards him.

"You only talked about this trail every day for the past two weeks. That or it could just be my natural-animal instinct." He smirked and leaned down once more to nuzzle her neck.

"Stop!" She shoved him away from her, listening for any sound that might indicate Cedar's promised return.

"Summer, what the fuck is your deal? I come out here looking for you, saving you, and this is my thanks?"

"I didn't ask to be saved. I didn't need to be saved, Harry. You can't be here. We can't," but she started to say, but was interrupted by Harry's bulging eyes as he looked past her. Summer turned to follow his gaze, already knowing what she would find.

Cedar stood some distance from them, still and silent.

"What the fuck is that!" Harry panicked and grabbed Summer's hand, yanking her towards him.

"Harry don't!" Summer pleaded. Cedar took a step towards them and let loose his fierce roar. Harry froze for a moment, his face turning pale as he stared into the deep dark hole of Cedar's open mouth, and the blaring teeth that lined it.

"Get the fuck away from us!" Harry screamed, switching into flight mode, turning to run and dragging Summer with him.

"Harry stop! He won't hurt us!" She looked back at Cedar pleadingly, finding him standing still and calm once more.

"The fuck it won't!" He pulled her harder, forcing her into the thickness of green that hugged the water's edge. Summer tried her best to resist, but could not muster the strength to stop Harry from pulling her with him as he crashed into the forest. He fought his way through as quickly as he could, swatting away branches with his free hand. Summer cycled between fighting Harry off and looking back for Cedar, but no sign of the giant creature was to be seen.

Harry continued racing with the river, following its flow until they soon came to where it narrowed and stopped resembling a lake, instead taking on its true nature as a river. The ground beneath them turned from forest floor to a rocky riverside as they stumbled around. The narrowing of the channel forced the river to surge with a newfound urgency. It beat against rocks and created a steady rush of sound as Harry continued using its downward flow as a compass. Summer frantically looked back once more, searching for any sign of Cedar. The fear of never seeing him again overcame her and tears fell from her eyes. This wasn't supposed to be the way they ended things.

"Harry, please," she cried, trying to compose herself.

The roar of the river became deafening, and Harry inadvertently led them to a large flat rock that stuck out, the river beside it free falling into a waterfall that easily outpowered the one Cedar and she had shared. Harry paused to peer down its steep drop, looking frantically around for any sign of a new path.

"This way!" He yanked on Summer's hand once more, attempting to lead her into the dark woods away from the river. He took two steps before he had to halt under the towering and immovable mountain that was Cedar, who had stepped forth from the forest blocking the path.

"I merely wish to say goodbye," Cedar spoke looking past Harry towards Summer's fearful face.

Shock from the unexpected speech registered on Harry's gaping face. Summer took the opportunity to jerk her hand free from his, rushing forward to fill the space between Cedar and Harry.

"Cedar," her eyes welled. "I'm so sorry." Her face contorted as she fought back tears.

Harry snapped from his shock and pulled Summer back once more.

"The fuck is this?" He bellowed looking between the Sasquatch and Summer. "You know this, this thing? Bigfoot? You're talking to fucking Bigfoot?" Harry's eyes flared in growing agitation, incredulous of the absolutely insane situation developing.

"He saved me," Summer smiled up at Cedar longingly.

Harry's anger masked the fear in his voice as he assessed Summer's stare.

"The fuck is going on?" He shouted louder to be heard over the raging falls behind him. "This is fucking bullshit. Summer we're leaving! I'm getting you out of this fucking forest and away from this Wookie!" He continued his attempt to tug her away, but she spun around swiftly, escaping from his grip.

"No!" She shouted, confidence and a newfound assurance lending her strength.

"I'm not going anywhere with you! I'm done Harry! Done with you! Do you understand that? I don't want to leave with you!" Her fury towards Harry shifted to a loving gaze as she looked back at Cedar.

"I'm staying here. With Cedar." She raised her hand towards Cedar for him to take.

The sound of a metal click locked Summer in place, and she quickly turned around to find Harry positioned with a handgun that was aimed directly at Cedar.

"Him? You'd rather fucking live out here, with this, this monster? You'd rather play homestead in the sticks with this beast over me!" The gun shook in his outstretched trembling hands as he yelled.

Summer raised her arms, taking a step towards Harry. "Harry, you don't understand. I love him. And," she looked over her shoulder at Cedar. "I'm sure he loves me." Cedar's lips curled to show an affectionate smile. She rounded on Harry, taking a step closer to him. "I'd rather live my life, out here, with him, than to ever have to imagine a life with you again! I'd rather live out here with a bear than with you!" The rushing water filled the awkward silence that had been created, and each member began calculating the next logical step in this wild interaction.

Harry reacted first. He laughed mockingly, a crazed look spreading over his face as he shook his head in disbelief.

"Well," he sighed out his last manic laugh. "Happily ever after to the both of you." Harry leveled the gun slightly higher before pulling the trigger. The ring of the shot cut into Summer's ears and finding its mark on Cedar's chest. Summer watched in horror as Cedar collapsed to his knees, clutching his heaving chest, his eyes wide and large nostrils flaring.

The click of metal sounded once more as Harry chambered another bullet. Summer's eyes flew wide as she shouted at Harry, "No! Stop!" The second shot split the air and rammed into Cedar's left shoulder, felling him onto his back, as he collapsed like a tree.

"Stop!" Summer screamed through tears as she watched Harry pull back the hammer of the gun. He took aim at the fallen creature for a third time.

100

"No!" Summer hurled herself at Harry shoving him back. Harry stumbled and tripped, misfiring the gun wildly into the air as his body fell off the flat rock and into the clashing falls below. Summer stared where Harry had just stood, unable to comprehend what she had just done.

A moan from Cedar brought her back to reality as she rushed to Cedar's side. Bright red blood pooled from the holes in his upper chest and shoulder. Summer shook her head, another wave of tears approaching as she watched the blood trickle into his jet-black fur.

"No, no, no. Please, please, I can't lose you too." She wept, using both her hands to lift his giant palm until it touched her face.

He peered up at her through half-opened eyes.

"Summer." His voice was hoarse and croaking as he brushed her cheek with his fingers.

She let out a desperate sob as she leaned her forehead to touch his. The image of Harry's body stumbling over the falls stirred inside her, emblazoned into her mind.

"I pushed him," her sobs came out in hot short breaths. "I pushed him over the edge and I, I killed him." The realization of her actions caught up to her. *I'm a murderer*, she told herself as her tears fell on Cedar's face. She knew then that she would never be able to return to the life and world that she once knew.

Once Harry's friends and family realized he was missing, she would definitely pose as the most likely suspect. Given the situation of her trip and his going after her, it wouldn't take much to convict her. *I'm just like Cooper*, she realized, her destiny sealed firmly forever in the forest.

"You saved me," Cedar croaked, lifting her wet face by her chin. "I may not experience love the way humans do. However," he coughed, clutching the seeping hole in his chest. "Seeing you, there next to the river…fear, an emotion I am not familiar with, caused me to realize, a life without Summer, brings no life. A life without you, would only mean eternal loneliness." He brought her face to his, gentle fingers still holding her chin, and began kissing her tenderly. Summer closed her eyes and kissed him back. He slowly let go of her lips and breathed the words into her: "I love you." Summer wrapped her arms around his furry head, holding on to him as if to never let go.

"Endings," he smiled weakly. "Only bring new beginnings."

While the water took no notice of this moment and continued to churn and chug its way over the ridge, somewhere in its watery depths filled with ancient rocks, and river algae, Harry's limp and crushed body was spun and kicked by the force of nature that answers only to gravity.

Chapter 13

Cedar walked slowly, hand in hand with Summer, as they entered the clearing where the stag had been shot. Dried mud and ground-up medicinal plants, mixed lovingly by Summer at Cedar's instructions, patched the two holes in his great body.

The body of the great stag had been scavenged by woodland predators. All that remained were several ivory bones, picked clean, and the stag's great antlers. Summer kneeled before them, her father's flask clutched in her hands.

"This is the best place to give him back to the Earth," Cedar stated, placing his hand on her shoulder. "To lay with my fallen friend, under the stars--a place you can always find him. He will forever be one with the forest." Cedar spoke ceremoniously as Summer dug a small hole next to the antlers.

"I love you dad," she whispered, unscrewing the lid and tipping the flask at an angle. Salt and peppered ash fell from the small container into the hole. Summer watched the steady stream, the only physical remains of father filling up the tiny piece of Earth that he would forever occupy. The flask soon emptied, and Summer scooped warm Earth to fill the hole. Patting the space gently, she took the nearest antler and placed it over the top.

"No endings," she said out loud. "Only new beginnings."

A distant, fearsome roar filled the sky at that moment. Summer jerked upright, looking around wildly for the source.

"What was that?" Summer asked Cedar with frightened eyes.

Cedar scanned the tops of the surrounding trees as another echoing bellow rose in the distance. He took Summer into hir arms.

"We will need to leave this place. I did warn you that I must travel often." His eyes darted from the trees to look down at Summer.

"Why? Because of that sound? What was that?" Summer looked into his great amber eyes searching his face for the truth.

He leaned down to kiss her, then let out a long sigh, heavy with tension.

"That," he said, looking out at the trees once more. "Was my first mate. And she is looking for me."